Soul Train

T. C. Husvar

Fulton Books, Inc.
Meadville, PA

Published by Fulton Books 2021

ISBN 978-1-63710-202-2 (paperback)
ISBN 978-1-63710-203-9 (digital)

Printed in the United States of America

Chapter 1

The Train Station

"UGH...MY HEAD," JOSHUA GRUMBLED as he felt a throbbing pain spiked through the side of his head. He winced as he brought a hand up into his thick, curly dark hair. The sound of a train squeal rang in his ears and caused him to open his dark-blue eyes. The coolness of the concrete ground emanated against him. People walked on the train platform around him and paid him no mind. The people were like a faceless, mindless sea. So many faces that Joshua felt a bit nauseous from the amount alone. A loud horn shouted out among everyone. The people grew still like machines that were being recalibrated. Slowly, people started to line up in front of a dark-colored train with a bright-red glow that came from the engine room at the very front.

"The hell?" Joshua felt another pang of pain shot through his head. He hissed as he used his arms and pushed himself up. It felt like a few tons of weight were all over his body as he tried to stand. He used all his might and pushed himself onto his knees. His head throbbed as another horn blared loudly. People pushed against his body to get in line. At first, his eyes glazed over the people that were all in matching clothes. Then he noticed his own sleeves and looked down at his clothes. They were different from what he remembered. A dark-gray jacket and pants with a darker button-down shirt. In fact, these clothes were soft against his skin. They looked and felt better than anything he had ever owned in his life. Last he remembered, he was in his jeans that were ripped apart by the dogs down his street as they chased him home from school. He had his favorite band T-shirt and jacket on from what he could remember.

At the sound of the third train horn, he felt his body move on its own and stir him out of his thoughts. He got onto his feet and started to follow the stragglers of people that fell into the back of a line. His eyes glanced around and saw other trains that people got on to, and each had multiple carts. There was a strange thing that Joshua picked up on. The people in his line all wore the same outfit. The people on different trains or carts had different versions of the same outfit on. Some had petticoats, others had heavier wool jackets, and some women had dark-gray dresses with bonnets on. Most, however, held blank expressions. It was almost like they were not even thinking about it. Some people were looking around, others looked sullen, and there were a few just like him, completely confused and lost.

"Tickets, get your tickets ready!" Joshua snapped ahead and saw a man, at least he thought was a man, waved with a big smile on his face. His voice was deep and musical as he called out for everyone to have their tickets. At that point, Joshua felt the beginning of a panic attack battle at his chest. He felt the familiar heart pace quickened and breathing shallowed. His palms immediately grew sweaty as he quickly patted down his pants pockets.

"Panic medication!" he hissed to himself as he always did. His fingers clawed along his new outfit for his medication. He shoved his hands into his pockets with the feeling of urgency as the line slowly dragged forward. He tried to get out of the line as he pulled at his pockets, but his feet refused to move. After a moment, the panic started to get worse. He finally felt something. A slick small piece of paper rubbed against his fingers. He pulled it out and saw a perfect-looking train ticket. It looked like something out of the 1950s movies that he watched as a kid. Big and shiny gold PP was stamped on his ticket with a spiky ball on the upper right-hand corner. Seeing a ticket in his hand, his panic started to slowly subside. He flipped the ticket over and saw that there was no price, train station logo, or really anything else on it. He continued to absentmindedly move up in the line as his eyes stared down at the ticket. The ticket was a phenomenon to him. He combed through his mind and could not remember ever purchasing a ticket. Then again, he also never bothered to take the train or subway before. The closest thing he had to a real train experience was picking up his uncle one time from a station. He was five though, and his mind was more on the salty pretzel stand that was behind him over the actual trains. The thought of soft, salty pretzels started to grasp at his attention after a moment, and his stomach grumbled.

"Ticket, please?" the dark, melodic voice stated as a pale white hand was flung into his face. Joshua was grabbed from his thoughts of food. He glanced back up in surprise to realize that he was at the front of the line. When he saw the man, his eyes widened. The man was so feminine even with such a deep voice. Joshua slowly handed the ticket as his eyes trailed over the man. He had a lithe, slim body that was noticeable even in the black suit with gold trimming on it. His hat covered up midnight hair that framed the man's face. His skin was as pale as alabaster. His eyes were a bright-silver color. His canines were also very prominent as he smiled and handed back the ticket. "Mr. Holmes! Any relation to Sherlock?"

Joshua slowly shook his head from side to side. "Oh, well. Please step aboard!" The man gave him back the ticket with a smile. Joshua slowly nodded. The man's smile seemed predatory to Joshua as he returned the smile and stepped inside. The entrance was bathed in a golden light. Scents of vanilla wafted in his nose as he walked into the golden-colored light that came from bulbs that were implanted into the ceiling. He turned to the right and saw a full cart of people as they sat around quietly. Some eyes stared back at him, which caused a bit of anxiety to spurt up inside him.

Do I look weird? he asked himself. His eyes remained on everyone as he stepped into the aisle and searched for an empty seat. Two seats about halfway down the aisle had yet to be taken. *Jackpot!* he thought. He snagged the seats and fell onto it with a tired sigh. Being around so many people always drained Joshua. Anything involving school was the worst of it for him. The smelly teenagers, drugged-out repeaters, and lazy teachers came to mind. His eyes glanced around the train again. *Well,* he thought, *better smelling people than high school, I guess.* The seat squeaked as he turned around and leaned back into it. A very small and fragile woman sat in front of him alongside a pale muscular man. The window called for his attention, and he indulged it with a single glance. Slowly, he watched the line move forward almost like a snail train. His eyes trailed toward the man in the suit again. Joshua saw the other passengers that came aboard got flustered by the man. The ticket rubbed against his palm as he held it and glanced down toward it. A thought popped up in his head as he looked it over carefully. His name was nowhere on this ticket.

"Do you mind if I sit next to you?" Joshua jumped a bit in his seat as he turned around and saw a frail elderly Asian woman smile down at him. He tried his best to give a noncreepy smile and nodded.

"Of course!" Joshua slightly shifted away from the woman as she took her time and got into her seat. She held on to her ticket with an iron grip, and what was written on it was not visible to him. She slid it into a pocket of her light-gray dress. Joshua crammed his into his pants pocket.

"So, dearie, how did you get on this lovely train today?" The woman turned to him, and her eyes glistened a bit at the thought of a conversation.

Joshua gulped. His hand scratched the back of his head with uneasiness. "I really don't know, to be honest." Joshua laughed nervously as the woman chuckled. "I don't even know where I am."

"Oh, I see. You know, I have taken this train before. I know exactly why we are on if you want to know."

Joshua felt his curiosity piqued. His attention homed in more on the woman. *She knows why we're here?* Joshua asked himself silently. "Where...where are we?"

"We are on the train that takes you around the parts of the world that the normal mind never sees prior to receiving their proper ticket!" She chuckled a bit as she shook her head. "It really is the ride of a lifetime."

"Proper ticket?" Joshua questioned.

"Let me see your ticket, sweetie." Joshua fished back out his ticket and held it out to her. She touched it with a gentle grip and read it. After a moment of silence, she nodded and motioned for him to put it away again. "Make sure that no one takes that ticket from you. That one is special."

Joshua's left brow raised to her. "Special how?" he asked.

"Teff will be able to explain it better than I can. It is your ticket after all. Everyone's ticket is special on here in different ways with different stops. I will tell you that you will not get off this train."

"I won't?"

Her head shook slowly as her smile grew gentler. "You will not. Be sure that you remember that. Call it grandma's intuition."

Joshua nodded after a moment, and she smiled sweetly at him. They went from the ticket to talking about life. She chatted about her children, grandchildren, and every animal that she ever owned in between. Joshua's shoulders sagged as he leaned back in his seat. The elderly woman glowed with fondness as she spoke. A sudden loud thud came from behind them, which stopped their conversation. She and Joshua looked back and saw the beautiful man walked into sight. Heads around them turned and looked toward the beautiful man. His sunshine smile charmed people as his eyes gazed at the crowded cart.

"Hello, everyone!" The song-like voice flowed through the whole cart as if there was a surround sound speaker. His feet slowly trailed to the front of the cart. "Welcome to the train ride of a life-time!" Joshua noticed the low chuckle from the grandma after the words were said. Uneasiness refilled his chest bit by bit like water in a cup. "There are only a few rules for this train ride. Your ticket will glow when you are meant for your stop! Please pay attention. Anyone with two Ps on it stays on the train the whole time. Now people will try to take your ticket. *Do not* let them! You do not want to deal with the station they have to stop at. And believe me, when some realize where they are going, they will do anything to find someone with that ticket." Joshua felt the ticket weigh down his pocket as the man walked by him. The man's silver eyes glanced at him for a brief moment as he continued. "I also recommend talking to the people on this train. A lot of people are wise here, and for anyone with that double P pass, it really is something worth listening to." When he got to the front of the train, he turned around with a ballerina's grace and clapped his hands. "Enjoy your ride! We will be leaving soon! We needed to refuel after the last ride, so it will take a minute."

A small little hand was raised in the front row. A wide-eyed girl came into Joshua's view when he craned his head. The man looked down at her, and his smile softened into something friendlier. He knelt to the girl and bowed with grace toward her. A giggle bubbled from the girl, and Joshua felt a smile crack across his face. "How may I be of help for thee, thy wonderful queen-to-be?" Joshua craned his neck further and saw the girl kick her legs since they did not reach the floor. She wore a fluffy pale-pink dress and a small little halo-like crown.

"You did not tell us your name, mister!" She giggled happily.

"Well, young queen-to-be, I am Teff. Teff the train conductor."

The girl nodded with a smile. "Well, it's great to meet you, Teff!"

"The pleasure is all mine," he said to her. He got back up on his feet. "If you need anything, you raise your hand and let me know, all right?"

Her curly hair bobbed as she nodded. Joshua heard the elderly lady chuckle beside him, and his head turned to her. "What's so funny?" he asked quietly.

"He has not changed one bit. Still a softie for children," the woman said fondly.

Joshua smiled. "So you know him?"

"A bit more than I would have liked," she admitted. There was no malice in her tone. In fact, it sounded a bit distant.

Did she just take this train recently? Joshua questioned to himself.

"Teff is not known for his…gentle approaches to anyone over the age of eighteen. He believes that anyone under that age was pushed to such limits that it is really not them to blame."

Joshua cocked his head a bit in surprise. "Blame?" Joshua asked. "Blamed for what? I'm only seventeen, and I don't even know why I'm here. Or how actually." The woman's face scrunched up and gave Joshua a pained expression. "I don't understand what's goin—" His sentence was cut off from a sharp pain to his head. His fingers intertwined in his hair as he grabbed at the spot. It throbbed on his head, and he groaned as he leaned forward a bit. Nausea ran through his system as he tried to take slow, steady breaths. He squeezed his eyes shut and concentrated.

"Here," the train conductor's deep voice said. "For the pain." Joshua saw the pale hand came into view as he opened his eyes. A bright-blue pill contrasted against the pale hand that held it. He grabbed the pill and gulped it down dry. After a few moments, the throbbing subsided, and pain dulled down. He glanced at the man's black-fingertipped hand that gently touched his own charming face that was lined with worry. "I don't think I have many of those pills for this trip. Let me know if you need another one though. You took one hell of a hit when you came here. Smacked your head right off the pavement."

Joshua nodded gratefully. "Thank you," Joshua said quietly. "I really appreciate it. Must be why I can't remember anything."

"No problem!" Teff smiled toward him and made his way back to the front of the train cart. A loud knock was heard from a door to the right in the front. Teff slightly opened it and peaked his head through. After a few moments of whispers that Joshua could not hear clearly, the door shut with a loud click of locks. At least three from what Joshua heard. Teff turned to the crowd with a huge smile, one that chilled Joshua to the bone.

"Great, we're leaving," Joshua whispered cautiously.

"All right, everyone! From the best to the worst, we are ready for our journey! I hope that everyone enjoys their ride and please hold on tight!" The sound of air hissed, and the roar of an engine caused the train to come to life.

Joshua felt a brand-new fear come to thought as he looked back at the train station. It was eerily quiet outside, and everyone that was lined up was gone. They had boarded onto their respective carts. A lump held tight in his throat. "Here we go." Joshua gulped.

Chapter 2

A Wonderful Trip Up!

THE TRAIN ROLLED OFF into a dawn-colored morning sky. Green pastures and different crops flew past them as the train chugged along. It was the countryside that Joshua had always wanted to see. Living in the inner city did not leave much to the imagination. This sure beat seeing homeless people curled up in alleyways, broken bottles and trash on the sidewalks, and different people staring at Joshua weird because he liked to dress a bit darker than everyone else. He hated dealing with the disgusting fumes of the city. In fact, the air here was cleaner, better for the body somehow as Joshua took in a deep breath. *I really need to get my writing career off the ground so I can move here,* Joshua thought. *No people, no fumes. Just me and nature. And maybe my sister.*

"So does anyone else know where we are? 'Cause I do not." The fragile woman turned around in her seat. Joshua nearly fell out of his seat when his attention turned to her. She had beautiful ginger-red hair and bright-green eyes. Her cheeks were a bit sunken in, but it brought out her cheekbones even more—a model in Joshua's eyes. He gulped down in his dry throat as he thought of something to say, anything to say. The woman beside him did not say anything. The woman smiled and shrugged her shoulders as she kept her hands on her lap.

"I don't," the man beside her said with a nonchalant shrug. "Eh, fuck it though. For some reason, we are all here. Just don't know why yet."

"Yeah, but isn't it weird that we don't know anything?" she asked. She rummaged in her seat, and her eyes widened a bit when she stilled. "Oh fuck, where's my phone?"

"Oh, sorry!" Teff said with a slight chuckle as he popped up beside her. "Phones are not allowed on this ride! They were taken away before you even got here."

Shock laced her face as she stared at the conductor. Her jaw fell to the floor and hands went limp to her sides. "What." It was not a question she asked it, and Joshua gently patted his pockets. His phone was not with him, and neither were his medication or asthma inhaler. Joshua felt trepidation in the pit of his stomach but did his best to dismiss it. *I'm so screwed* was all he thought as he stared back at the conversation.

"Train policy," Teff explained.

"I just bought that phone last week!" the girl burst out. Both the conductor and Joshua's eyes widened at the outburst. "How can I *not* have it?"

Teff clicked his tongue against his teeth a few times as he shook his head. His fake sympathy would normally be comical to Joshua if he were not so close to the girl. Teff started to walk down the aisle. "Sorry! Nothing lasts forever. You'll get over it."

The girl jammed her elbow on the armrest and held her head in her hand as she brooded silently. Joshua glanced over at the man beside her. He shrugged to himself and leaned back in his own seat. His eyes went toward the window.

"I *cannot* believe that I will not be able to talk to my followers until the end of this," she scoffed quietly. Joshua's ears perked at the sound of whistling. He turned his head and saw the conductor as he whistled and chatted with other patrons. Joshua heard a low chuckle and snapped his head back forward.

"Followers? Really? That is your concern?" The man beside her scoffed as he turned to her. Joshua leaned forward and nodded.

"Yeah, I feel like that should be the last thing to worry about right now," he added in. The two men looked at each other and fist-bumped as a greeting.

The woman only stared between the two and then rolled her eyes hard enough that Joshua felt it himself. Irritation radiated from the girl as she clicked her tongue. "You wouldn't get it."

"How old even are you? You look like you are well over fifteen, which is above the normal age for girls to be screaming for their phones," the man beside her asked casually. He tipped his chair back a bit and rested his right foot on the edge.

"I'm not that young," she bit back with a scowl lining her brow.

"That also does not answer my question," he replied back coolly. Joshua glanced over at the elderly woman as she slowly shook her head. She glanced over to him and gave him a sad smile.

"Twenty-five." The girl cringed a bit. "What about you?"

"Twenty-two." They looked back at Joshua and the elderly lady. "What about you two?"

"Oh, I'm only seventeen." Joshua nervously chuckled a bit as he sank in his seat.

"Ninety-two!" The elderly woman perked up at the number. "Oh-ho, I win!" Joshua smiled at the woman's optimism. The other two chuckled and turned more toward them. "What did you do for the interweb, dearie?" Joshua and the other guy chuckled at the word *interweb*. *Dad says that,* Joshua thought.

"Oh, I uh, showed people eating habits. You know, simple stuff," the woman said, a bit shier. She cleared her throat, and her eyes cast downward.

"Oh, but you are so tiny!" The woman frowned in concern. "Hopefully, you are given a chance to correct it." Joshua looked back at the elderly woman and saw that hopeful gleam in her eye. "You need some meat on your bones." The redhead looked back up shyly at the comment.

"A-actually, I'm a vegan. Meat has too many calories."

"Calories?" The old woman scrunched up her nose. "You sound just like my youngest granddaughter Rieko. She is such an intelligent girl, but she cares too much about her body. She is so, so beautiful just like you, but she is so thin! She needs to eat more as well. You and her would probably get along!"

Joshua smiled a bit at the girl's shy smile.

"You think I'm beautiful?" the girl asked.

"Of course!" The elderly woman's elbow jabbed lightly into Joshua's arm. "And I'm sure this young man here agrees!"

Joshua's cheeks flushed as he looked toward the girl's expectant eyes. He nodded. "Y-you are beautiful," Joshua said as he cleared his throat.

The girl's cheeks turned a slight rose color as the elderly woman spoke up. "What is your name, dearie? I am sure it is just as pretty as your face!"

The girl's smile brightened as she turned back to the elderly woman. "Madeline."

"Oh, how wonderful," the woman said with a soft smile. She turned to the boy next to her. "And your name, young man?"

The guy sat up in his seat and turned to see her. "Jason."

The woman turned to Joshua next. "And you, sweetie?"

"Joshua."

The four of them felt themselves being sent backward into their seats by a huge force. The train picked up speed, and Joshua heard the chugging from the train as it grew louder. His heart pace quickened a bit. The small chatter that livened the cart died down into silence as they felt themselves being pushed back against the seats harder from the momentum. Teff sauntered along the aisle of the cart with ease. When he got to the front of the cart, he placed his hand on the wall just barely above his head and pressed in. A square just barely bigger than his hand pressed inward. He slid it up and revealed a shiny golden-yellow bell. He grabbed the golden string that hung from the bottom of the bell and turned around with a bright smile. "Everyone, get ready! We are going into the exosphere!"

Joshua squinted his eyes as he looked out to the pastures as they passed. "The hell?" Joshua heard Jason ask quietly.

"You know, it's been a minute since I've been in science class, but isn't that in outer space?" Joshua asked as he leaned forward. Jason slowly nodded.

"Yeah, and I thought we were going to hell first too," Jason murmured back.

"Hell?" Joshua asked.

Suddenly, the train lurched onto the tracks. Joshua held on to his seat with a deathlike grip as the rest of the cart started to murmur. A tense air formed among the crowd as it jumped. Joshua glanced around the cart. Teff and the elderly woman he was next to seemed rather calm as everyone else's eyes grew wider and wider. Joshua felt his own breath turn shallow as he turned out the window. They were close enough to the front of this steam engine and saw the tracks a bit in front of them. His heart fell into his stomach as he saw half of the track split off toward the right. There was no other half to the track. It looked perfectly cut in half to him.

"We are gonna die," Joshua whispered in fear under his breath.

"Die? Sweetie, calm down, everything is all right." The elderly woman's attempt at comfort fell on deaf ears as he continued to watch. The train jumped again as if trying to free itself from the tracks. Joshua felt a light touch on his shoulder and turned to the woman that gave him quiet reassurance. He tried to clear the lump in his throat as he stared back out the window. They were getting really close to the split track, and his heart was ready to jump out of his chest. He did his best to shut off his heart as he sunk even further into his seat.

The train jumped again, and he felt momentum wanting to push him down. His heart pounded, eyes widened, and he glared out and saw that the train was off the ground. He saw the tracks split below him and went in opposite directions. Green pastures below him got smaller and smaller. Golden barrels of hay in the farther distances became small specks. Joshua felt his soul leave his body from the fear. The farther away he went, the smaller he felt. His hand pulled at his dark curly hair. The pain surged through him and reminded him to ground himself. Slowly, he took deeper and deeper breaths. The sounds of the train came to life as the tints of blue sky and clouds took over his view. The fears and complaints of other passengers filled his ears.

"Don't worry, don't worry!" Teff's cheerful voice stated as he went back to walking back up and down the aisle. It reminded Joshua of more of a prison guard over a train conductor. "It's no different than taking an airplane ride! Or a rocket ship if you have had the pleasure."

"We are supposed to be on a *train*!" Madeline spoke up as she stood on her feet. Her face was blotchy and red as she stared at Teff. Fire flamed in her eyes. Another fact seemed to appear to Joshua as he watched the fiery girl. She was thin. In fact, she probably could not pass for a paperweight. The bones poke out of her chest, and the skin clung to her fingers as she extended her angry fingers out. He looked at Teff's hands in comparison. He was rather slim as well, but his skin did not cling to him as it did to her. Sadness pinged at his heart as he watched Teff calm Madeline down. She sat with a loud huff. The entire cart watched the two interact. Teff did his best to maintain his composure. Joshua noticed the twitch in the conductor's brow as he tried again to tell Madeline to calm down.

"Dearie," the elderly woman finally stood up and touched her shoulder from above her seat. "Calm down, it is not that scary." Madeline whipped her head back toward the woman.

"W-what do you mean? We are in the sky! Heading to *space*!"

"I know it seems scary, but do not get upset at Teff. He is only here to make us all comfortable while we go on this journey. Keep in mind, this is a ride of a lifetime."

Madeline gawked back at the woman confused, but the reassuring smile was enough for Madeline, who slowly nodded and turned back to Teff. "I'm sorry," Madeline mumbled toward Teff.

Teff gave his best charming smile. "It is not a problem. I know that some people get scared over the silliest things. Is that not what makes life worth living, though? Facing those fears?"

Madeline nodded timidly as she sank further into her seat. Joshua looked back outside and saw the clouds that surrounded them as they went further and further up. Soon, the blueness of the sky started to fade out as well as the clouds. There was a huge jump of the train. Pitch darkness started to bleed into the surroundings, and white tiny spheres glowed around them. He noticed that some of those white spheres moved and connected below and ahead of them. "Star track?" Joshua asked as he looked out the window.

"Yeah, and our stop does not seem to be that far away," Jason stated as he pointed to somewhere beyond the window. Joshua squinted his eyes and saw a small star that seemed to outshine the rest not far from where they were chugging along at. After a few moments, he picked out that it was actually a nebula, and some lights glimmered around the nebula. They were similar to runway lights from airports in Joshua's eyes.

"That's insane. And I thought Hollywood glowed," Joshua said in awe.

The sound of humming had Joshua snap his head in the direction of Teff. He had a black pocket watch out, and it slowly ticked away. Teff formed a thin smile on his lips. "Perfect," he heard Teff say. "We are just on time!" The distinct click of the pocket watch as it closed was clear to Joshua's ears. The man seemed almost otherworldly already with how relaxed he was. Joshua turned himself and looked back out into the starry atmosphere. His eyes lowered down and past the starry tracks that formed beneath them. There was nothing beneath them except the earth itself, which was miles away.

"Wow, it's so lonely when you look at how small it is in space," Joshua mumbled to himself. "Almost like home." Even on this train with different people, even with a semicrazy train conductor, and even with no reason at all to feel so. The looming loneliness that he would always experience at school and home crashed down like a tsunami wave. The depression that he had been fighting for years almost seemed irresistible currently. He had no idea why he was here. In fact, it seemed that no one really did other than the woman next to him. His anxiety had been at a ten compared to the normal day-to-day five. The only good thing was that the headache was over for a while. He tried to think again about where he was prior to the station. No recollection of ever wanting to take a train ride ever came to thought although he did not regret it completely. When the slight pang of a headache started to resurface, he groaned internally and turned to the station that they slowly rolled toward.

Chapter 3

First Stop!

ALL THE FEARS THAT most people had being in outer space stopped as soon as they pulled up toward the nebula. A new sense of wonder and excitement fell over everyone as they got closer to the station. The nebula that was in the distance started to look more like a station that led into a utopia-like metropolis. Glittering large buildings showed off in the distance as they all pulled into a white station with a rainbow hue that reflected off everything. Joshua could not believe his own eyes. A nebula as a whole cityscape was breathtaking to everyone on board. Small murmurs erupted as everyone watched people in all-white clothing walked onto the station from other trains that were parked on different platforms. Some seemed to have gold wings shining from glittery jackets, while others did not. A broad smile formed on Joshua's face. This place brought off a vibe of happiness and purity inside him.

"Seems too good to be real, huh?" Joshua's ears perked up and turned to the elderly woman. Her eyes twinkled as she stared at the scenery past the boy.

"It sure is beautiful. Where are we?"

The woman chuckled a bit. Her smile softened as she looked back at Joshua. "The first stop, of course! We are at station HN."

"HN? What does that mean?"

"Oh, I'm sure that Teff will explain it all to you at some point."

They all heard the sounds of air rushed out as the train parked and a loud horn sounded from outside. The elderly woman had a sparkling smile as she pointed past Joshua. He turned and saw her finger pointed at a man that stood on the platform. His hair was thinned at the top, and Joshua saw the wrinkles that cracked on his face. He had an excited smile and was waving at the train with anticipation.

"Who's that?" Joshua asked.

"That's Arnold, my husband." Excitement laced her voice as she spoke. "I knew he would wait for me."

"Aw, that's so sweet," Joshua commented.

"Passengers!" Teff's voice had everyone stop their conversations and look up to the train conductor. "Here is stop HN! For everyone that has a glowing ticket, please hold on to it, and one of the guardians will be with you shortly! Remember, this is for the people that have HN on their tickets and glow really bright!" His smile was cheery and refreshing as he walked toward the back of the cart.

Joshua looked over to the woman as she pulled out her ticket. The ticket came to life. It glowed a bright white with a rainbow-like reflection on it. The HN stood out in a blinding white color. Her hand gripped it tightly as she pulled it up to his eyes' view. "Wow," he said, amazed.

"This is what a ticket does when it is signaling the right station. That way, no one could get off at the wrong station."

Joshua nodded. Jason and Madeline turned around and stared at the ticket in curiosity. "So my ticket will do the same thing?" Madeline asked. She pulled out her ticket and flipped it around. A frown graced her beautiful features as she turned it every which way. "This one doesn't glow! What gives?"

Jason pulled out his ticket next. "I guess we aren't special," he chided. "Mine isn't glowing either. But then again, it doesn't have HN on it. It has like HL 1." He held it up and stared at it. The yellow light of the train was all that reflected off the lifeless ticket. He shrugged as he brought the ticket back down. He shoved it in his pocket and grumbled, "Guess I couldn't get any better than hell after all." Joshua barely heard it when he strained his ears.

Madeline examined the writing of her ticket closely. The ticket dropped her interest. "Same here. Mine says HL 5B," she commented. The ticket was shoved back into her pocket.

"Haha, mine's a one. I'm better," he added cheekily. His grin grew on his face as Madeline growled at him.

"Weird, I wonder if all these stations look this cool," Joshua commented. His eyes glanced at the elderly woman and saw a frown fell on her face for a brief moment before the sound of a door being opened caught her attention. Everyone looked back, and four different men walked onto the train. They all had on crisp white suits with golden wings pinned on the right side. Each man looked beautiful just like Teff, yet they had a different air that surrounded them. It was warm and loving, almost like a warm blanket to Joshua. Each one stopped at a glowing ticket. The elderly woman got a dark-skinned man with a glowing white smile. He had two sets of wings on his white shirt, and Joshua's brows quirked.

"Oh! You have two sets of wings! That must mean something special!" The elderly woman squealed in delight. The man chuckled to her and held out his hand.

"It only means that I was a veteran. I served for the United States Army," he explained proudly.

Joshua perked up at the comment. "That's amazing! Thank you for your service!" Joshua exclaimed.

The man smiled brightly at him and nodded. "Thank you for giving me a reason to serve. I spent twelve years serving and loved every moment with the infantry." His gaze went back down to the woman. "Are you ready to go, ma'am? I know you have a man out there that has been waiting for your special heart for sometime now." The elderly woman took his hand with a firm grip, and he helped her up.

"With him by my side, I'll have the strength of ten soldiers." She chuckled as she handed him her ticket.

"Thank you, ma'am." He looked at the glowing ticket and put it in his pocket. She looked at Teff as he made his way through. When he reached the elderly woman, he paused. A sigh escaped his lips and nodded to her. "It will be a shame seeing you go." Joshua heard the genuineness of the comment. "I hope you enjoyed *both* rides on the train."

The woman nodded her head as gratefulness glittered in her eyes. "You helped me get back on a better path, Teff. I owe you so much."

"And you repaid it by fixing your life. For that, I am proud to have been your conductor." He stood up straighter and stepped aside with an exaggerated arm extended. Teff went up to the little girl next. She had a gentle-looking woman at her side that almost glowed as she smiled down to the girl. Teff looked down at the girl with a soft smile. He knelt to her and ruffled her hair. She giggled and gave him a hug. "And if this girl is ever mean to you, you come back to me and I'll straighten her up, my queen-to-be."

She laughed as she looked back at the train conductor. "She's really nice, Teff! She said she was taking me to a crowning tea party!"

His smile was sad even with her being filled with glee. He nodded to her. "Well then, you are officially my queen. And I am glad I could serve you."

"Thank you, Teff!"

"My queen," her guardian interrupted, "you are going to be late if we do not hurry!"

Her smile widened as she turned back to Teff. "I gotta go, Teff!"

"Of course, my queen." He bowed to her and stood. She ran off the train with her guardian in tow. Joshua felt his heart warmed at the moment. When he looked at the conductor, he seemed sad. But it only lasted a moment before he smiled again. When the last of them got off the train, everyone heard the door shut with a soft click. Joshua felt his pulse as it nearly jumped out of him. Questions pounded through his mind at a rapid-fire rate. His mind immediately quieted down at the sound of the bell as it rang from its spot above Teff. He had a devilish glint in his eye as they heard the train roared back to life. "That was delightful, wasn't it?" Teff kept up his songlike voice as the train groaned with anticipation to go. Joshua and a few others nodded in agreement. He chuckled a bit as he rang the bell again. "Well, off we go! To our next adventure!"

Joshua peered out the window as the train crawled at an agonizingly slow rate. His attention caught a glance at the elderly woman with the man that waited outside for her. They were kissing and hugging with smiles on their faces as they became inseparable from each other. The veteran with them laughed at something the woman said. Joshua smiled at the trio. They were cute together. As they rolled from his sight, he silently wished her good luck and safe traveling to wherever they went. As they pulled from the station, the star track slowly trailed them downward to earth again. Part of him felt a major relief by this. Earth was a nice planet. He wanted to be back there and out of the exosphere. Yet there was something nagging at the back of his mind like there always was. *Why are we going back down to earth?*

Chapter 4

Sea Level!

JOSHUA'S FINGERS DRUMMED AGAINST his armrest as they steadily made their way back down to earth. The questions steadily grew to the forethought of his mind. The stars around him gave little interest but did give him something to look at as they went down. The train hummed along smoothly even for being in the sky. *At least I won't get airsick from turbulence,* he thought. His eyes went from one to another with a newfound interest as he sat up. He remembered when he was younger and his grandmother would tell him that every star was an angel looking down on a person. He remembered her telling him to pray to the stars because they were angels in disguise. When he was older and school taught him differently, he was shocked at first and heartbroken. And when he told his grandmother, she shrugged him off and said that God did not have to explain why He hid them the way He did.

Her death a few years ago devastated him. As he watched her casket get rolled away for the final time hit him harder than the wake ever did. He was fourteen, and he remembered holding on to his mother like a lifeline throughout the funeral. A tear pricked at the edge of his eye as he remembered her. He reminisced on looking up the stars at night after night for months after the funeral. He had so many questions, so much he did not understand. Concepts that he still did not grasp. He pondered if she ever watched him and if she ever missed him. After a sigh, he wiped away the tear that threatened to escape his eye. It was not something to think about now, yet he had no choice but to think about it. He felt the presence of someone to his immediate left and heard someone sit down. He whipped his head over to the person that sat down next to him.

"Sorry," the person mumbled as they sat down. Joshua stared at the person for a moment. The person had long dark hair and wore a skirt. Yet at the same time, they had an Adam's apple jutting from the throat. The person stared back at him after a moment and waved shyly. They shifted their dark-framed lenses to get a better view of him. "Can I help you?" the person questioned sternly.

Joshua shook his head. "N-no. Just...sorry...wasn't expecting you to sit down next to me," Joshua stuttered to get out.

"Was that *all* you weren't expecting?" The person quirked a brow to him.

Joshua opened his mouth but clamped it shut tightly. After a moment, embarrassment brightened his cheeks as he looked away. "Sorry..." he muttered quietly.

"No, I'm sorry," the person said. Joshua looked back at the person. "Without my makeup on, I know that I don't fully look like who I really am." Joshua nodded. "My name is Tiffany. What's your name?"

"Joshua." He opened his hand out to the person, and they shook with a friendlier smile.

"Her/she by the way," the person said with a glint in their eye.

"I'm sorry?" Joshua asked.

"My pronouns. I'm she." Joshua's eyes trailed over her and saw the more feminine figure after a moment. "Like what you see?" She giggled.

Joshua cleared his throat as his beet-red cheeks returned. "S-sorry. That's cool by the way," he shakily stated. "So do you know why we're all here?" She shook her head and moved some of her hair that better showcased her brilliant brown eyes and alabaster skin. Joshua snapped his fingers as he slouched back in his chair. "No one seems to know."

"Same with where I was sitting too," Tiffany commented.

"Good to see that we are all in the same boat!" Jason quipped as he turned around in his seat and waved toward the woman. "I'm Jason."

"Tiffany," she said, and her eyes glittered more at the sight of him. "You're cute!" Jason chuckled as his dark-green eyes shined. He moved back some of his wispy dark hair and leaned closer to her. "You got a job, handsome?"

"I, uh…well, I mean I did."

"Oh yeah? What was that?" Tiffany leaned forward in her seat and propped her elbow on her knee and rested her head in her hand. Sparks flew between the two as they idly chatted.

Joshua leaned forward alongside them to try to add to the chat. An awkwardness rose in his chest, however, and remained as a silent onlooker. The conversation flooded into his ears, and surprise filled him as he listened. Jason, apparently, was a bad boy in the most generic sense to Joshua. A wannabe drug dealer that got hooked up in a gang. A high school dropout. He also had three children that he did not claim. All that was the exact opposite of Tiffany. She admitted that she always wanted to dress and be like a girl ever since she was little. She would be more into fashion and styles over watching cartoons or playing sports. She came out to her parents at sixteen, and they immediately cast her out. She stayed at different halfway houses until she was nineteen and had enough money for her own place. She was working to get enough money to get her GED and make her way to college to become a plastic surgeon. Her words stated her passion to help other people like her and create safer procedures at a cheaper cost.

"Wow, that's amazing," Jason admitted as he listened intently.

"Yeah," Tiffany said as blush dusted her cheeks, "I thought so too. Seeing how expensive treatments are, it's so unfair! How can someone like me ever afford to be who I really am when the prices are outrageous! I want to create something safer and cheaper for people like me. No one should ever have to live in a skin that they don't feel like is their own. In a body that clearly isn't them! Right?"

"Yeah!" Madeline stated loudly as she turned to Tiffany. "I'm right there with you, girl!" The two women high-fived as they smiled at each other. "I want to support your movement! When we get off this train, I am so posting about this!" Tiffany giggled happily.

"You really are inspiring, Tiffany," Joshua added.

"Oh, please! Call me Tiff. I prefer that anyways," she said as she waved him off.

"All right, Tiff," Joshua corrected. "Still, your idea is amazing! I think that with a little support, you could easily go a long way!"

"Thanks, I hope so too." She smiled at him, and Joshua saw the woman that Tiff was. A beautiful woman with a caring soul. Madeline grabbed Tiff's attention about makeup advice, and Joshua leaned back out of conversation. He admitted to himself long ago that makeup was Sophie's thing, and he would never understand it. When Joshua looked back outside, the stars faded into a dark-blue sky. He saw a flat stretch of sea that they headed toward. The dark blue turned into a light blue with puffy clouds surfaced up around him. For a moment, he thought he was on a plane getting ready to land. His attention glanced back at the rest of the people on the cart, and they were busy carrying on with their own conversations.

"So what is your life like outside of here, Joshua?" Joshua snapped back into the conversation with a small huh. "Your life? Outside of here?" Tiffany asked again.

"Oh, well, I guess there isn't much to tell. I am a high schooler. I mean, I am only seventeen. And I just got laid off from my job bagging groceries at my local Quick-E Mart. Um, other than that, I guess I'm just kind of a loner. I mean...I'm just the quiet kid. I get picked on every now and then, but it's whatever, ya know?"

Tiffany nodded to him. "Yeah, I get that. I used to be that way when I was Derrick. I got bullied a lot for it too," Tiffany admitted quietly.

"You too?" Joshua asked in shock. "But you seem so nice!"

"Doesn't mean that being different was a perk in my school. I'm a Midwest kid. You don't...we don't do change where I come from. Not my kind of change anyways."

Joshua chewed on his lower lip nervously as he nodded. "I'm sorry about that, Tiffany. I wish you were where I'm from. We would be loners together."

≣≣≣≣≣ 25 ≣≣≣≣≣

Tiffany gave him a small smile. "Yeah, I agree. We would have been great friends. But hey, it wasn't all bad. My boyfriend is hot as hell. And I do a bit of dancing. Honestly, I enjoy my life."

"I'm glad. Wish I could say the same. The best I ever got to do was marching band if you consider that dancing." Tiffany laughed at Joshua, and her smile lit up his face. "Hey, don't knock it till you try it! It's hard!"

"I'll believe it when I see it." Tiffany chuckled. "Still, even though I've been disowned, kicked out, and had to work my way up, I have someone that loves me supporting me, and I don't regret a moment of my life. Not one."

Joshua nodded. *I did though,* he thought.

They stared at each other for a long moment with awkward smiles before they turned their attention away from each other. Joshua's eyes darted at Jason and saw his frown as he turned around. Madeline lost interest quickly after and turned in her seat. He went back to looking out the window. He saw that they got closer to the sea. At the sight of that, his heart skipped a beat, and he tried to breathe in deeply. The last thing he needed was a panic attack in the middle of a train full of strangers. His hands gripped his seat so tight he swore that he was leaving scratch marks for the next passenger.

"We are hitting the water?" Tiffany asked as she glanced out past Joshua. He slowly nodded in response as his complexion turned wan. "Joshua? You okay?" Her hand waved in his face. Joshua's lungs did their best to remember how to breathe to calm the heart that pounded between his ears. After a moment, he felt hands touched his face and forced him to look at Tiffany in her dark eyes. "Joshua. Focus on me." His head nodded numbly as his gaze pinned on her. "Tell me your favorite color."

"What?" Joshua asked. Confusion scrunched up his facial features.

"Favorite color. Now." Her voice left no room for judgment.

Joshua thought for a moment. "Blue," he said with shallow breath.

"Favorite car?"

Joshua darted his eyes to her hairline for something to focus on. After a moment, his heart stopped pounding as loud. "Ferrari."

"Why?"

"Because it's a sports car." His eyes straightened on her again. "And you cannot tell me that they do not deserve some praise for being able to come up with those sleek designs." His breath normalized, and his heart subsided into a steady drum.

"So you like cars?" Tiffany asked as she let her grip soften around his face.

"Don't you?"

"Not nearly as much. I'm more of an artsy girl myself."

"Car designing can be artsy!" Joshua protested.

Tiffany let go of his face with a smile. She listened as Joshua passionately told her about how different car layouts could be seen as its own art form. She nodded and hummed on cue but overall did not interrupt him. When he was done, she agreed with his argument and had no real rebuttal to it. "Feel better?" she asked cautiously after a moment of silence.

Joshua thought for a moment, and in reality, he felt like the weight had been lifted off his shoulders. He nodded. "What was that you did?" he inquired.

"My little sister has anxiety too," she said softly. "She doesn't have medicine for it, so we came up with this questionnaire sheet that she would answer to get her mind off it. When her eyes light up, I know I hit the right topic for that day, and I have her go into depth on it. Kinda like I just did with you."

"Wow, that's helpful. Thanks!" Joshua praised. "You are super smart."

"Thanks." Tiffany's cheeks turned crimson at the compliment. "I appreciate it."

Joshua nodded. They sat back in comfortable silence for a moment. The immediate inertia lunged from hitting the water and caused both of them to lurch forward in their seats. They hit the back of the seat in front of them, while Madeline and Jason toppled onto the ground. Joshua groaned as his head whiplashed. He pushed himself back into his seat and turned his head and saw Tiffany do the same. "Are you okay?" he asked as he heard the chorus of groans from the rest of the cart. She nodded but remained silent. Joshua turned to the window and saw that they sat idly on top of the ocean water. Waves shot up in the far distance, but nothing was headed their way. He heard the water move underneath and against the train. His eyes gazed back at Tiffany and saw that she stared over at Teff. Teff walked through the seats in the aisle and halfheartedly made sure that everyone was okay. When he got to their seats, he gazed at them and kept moving. Madeline huffed and crawled back onto her seat.

"Thanks for the warning, *train conductor*," she sarcastically grumbled as she stretched. "That hurt."

"All right, everyone! We are at our next stop! Anyone have a ticket with a P on it? Nothing else, just a P! We are at station P!" Teff sang to the crowd. Joshua chuckled childishly as he swung his head back and saw that two people had tickets that glowed and held them up for him to see. "Well then, step on up! Step on up!" He beckoned them to the front of the cart. The two people, both men that seemed to be in their late forties, got up. There was no real expression to their faces and trailed up to the front like zombies. Joshua took a sharp intake of breath as he remembered them in the latest video game he played about zombies that took over the world. "All right, hand me your tickets!" He stuck out his hand to the both of them. Their glowing tickets dropped into his hand, and he stuffed them in his pocket. After that, his body turned to his left and opened an emergency door. Joshua watched as the conductor said something low for only the two up front to hear. They nodded to him and started for the open door. Joshua watched intrigued like everyone else on the cart. When they got to the door, they took one step out, and everyone gasped.

Joshua's face turned into one of horror as he watched. Tiffany gripped his arm in shock. The man started to dissipate into particles. A wind carried his particles away until there was nothing left. As the next guy went toward the door, the rest of the cart shouted out for him not to. No one understood what was going on. Jason got up in an attempt to physically stop the man from the door but was stepped down by Teff in the process and barricaded him to his seat. The man walked to the door and disappeared the same way the first man did.

This alone caused an uproar of panic to start in the train cart. Some screamed in horror, others gasped, and some even sobbed, while others remained silent onlookers. Madeline sat motionless at the sight before her, while Jason slumped back in shock as Teff moved away from him. Tiffany held on to Joshua's arm with a loosening grip, while Joshua stared at Teff in confusion. He was perfectly cool and collected among the chaos of the cart. He even looked a bit pleased with himself as he watched over the display before he shut the door. Teff let the cart turn into a stunned silence on their own before he opened his mouth. He had a comical look on his face as he watched the crowd before he spoke. Joshua could not even process the events in his head, but he knew that Teff could make sense of it. He was the train conductor after all. *That elderly woman said so anyways,* he thought.

"Ladies and gentlemen! I don't see why you are all being so fretful. This is the train ride of a lifetime after all!" He chuckled comically as he stared at his shocked audience.

"What the hell! They don't seem to be *alive* for the lifetime event anymore!" an older woman from the back of the cart shouted toward Teff. Teff cackled openly. Joshua's gaze stared at him in pure shock.

"Are you insane?" Jason questioned out loud.

"What even happened to that person?" a woman somewhere behind Joshua asked.

"Hm?" Teff stopped his laughter and stared at the front door. He gave himself a moment to calm down before he turned back to the crowd. "Oh, all right. Your reactions are so priceless that it is worthy of an explanation." He leaned back against the front of the cart and crossed his arms. A wide smile spread over his face that sent chills down Joshua's spine. "Like I said, this is a ride of a lifetime. But what you all take as me being extra, I say in all seriousness! You all are on, what we call in the afterlife, the soul train." The train groaned as it settled. Tension flooded the cart as the words left the conductor's lips. Joshua's stomach churned as if he were going to throw up. Tiffany dropped her grip on him, and it fell uselessly at her side.

"W-we're dead?" Madeline's whisper broke the silence but could barely utter the words as they left her lips. Teff's eyes twinkled with a sly smile before he continued.

"Well, most of you are dead. A few of you are actually in limbo. Meaning you are in coma or a near-death situation that you aren't awake from yet, and you got a free test ride on this train. It happens to the best of us sometimes. Suicide attempts, almost homicides, things of that nature." He waved his hand off at the very thought. "A useful waste of a ticket if you ask me."

"S-so those guys…" a man trailed off from somewhere in the middle of the train.

"We are currently in what you all call purgatory. The P on the ticket stands for purgatory." He clasped his hands in a bit of delight. "Oh, all of your faces are just so precious right now! The shock is finally settling down, and understanding is flooding throughout all of you of where you're actually at."

"You're sick!" someone called out.

"What happened to those men?" another asked aloud.

"What the hell are these tickets?" a man questioned angrily.

"Where were we just at then?" a younger female voice trembled as she asked.

Teff chuckled at all the questions with a certain playfulness in his eyes, a thing that terrified the air right out of Joshua. "What happened you ask? Well, they are, what you all would know it as, reincarnated. Purgatory is for the purely neutral. They cannot be defined by heaven or hell, so what happens is that they are dropped back off on earth. They turn back into the universal energy that we all use to live and thrive off of, and their souls return to another human life cycle to be rejudged, so to speak. The cycle will continue until they can clearly be defined as one or the other. Isn't it fascinating?" No one moved to answer. Everyone's silence showed that they were enraptured by the explanation. "Now as for our last stop, well, we were in heaven of course! Those men with winged pins were guardian angels of the souls that were previously on this train! They were taking their passengers to the waiting area so that they could get their wings and watch over the next humans birthed. It is an enthralling cycle to watch!"

"Why didn't you tell us this when we started the journey?" The question blurted out of Joshua's mouth before he even had time to think. Teff glanced at him with a curious eye before his smile dimmed.

"Even the quiet one speaks," he heard Teff muttered softly. "Well," he said aloud, "there is an obvious reason as to why!"

"What reason could you ever have to—" Madeline's question was interrupted by his raised hand. The mirth in his expression showed his entertainment in the reactions of everyone. Madeline's shoulders turned rigid as she quietly shut her lips together.

"Sadly, heaven has rules. They require their angels be with the ones that they watched over and were meant for heaven and would find it very disheartening if they found out someone stole a heavenly or purgatory ticket. So they require us to stay quiet until those passengers have safely exited. I love my job. I'd rather not lose it by not following the rules! Wouldn't you agree?"

"But why are you able to tell us now then?" Tiffany spoke up.

The gleam in Teff's eyes turned dark, and his smile grew nightmarishly large. His chuckle was dark and bone-chilling as he looked around the room. "Because hell has far fewer rules. Past this point, you all are going to the same place, granted in different parts of it. You all are categorized by your ticket on which layer of hell and substation that you are dropped off at after this. Some of you may want to barter or trade for a lighter sentence, but the only way any of you could do that is by finding someone else's ticket with a lighter sentence and stealing it before they even realize it's missing! When it glows with that person, then that is it! That is where you go!"

"So there is no way for us to get sent somewhere outside of hell," Madeline stated grimly.

"Oh, my dear, I never said that either. You need to learn to listen. Listen!" Teff tapped his ears. Joshua felt his heart skip a beat.

"But you said heaven and purgatory have rules," Madeline countered.

"I also said there were some near deathers on board as well," he said with a malicious chuckle. "And those near deathers go back to their bodies almost as fast as they left them. You are all in a state where time has no boundary and can be controlled far too easily." Joshua shivered at the tone of voice. "On this specific cart, you have two very lucky individuals. Find their tickets and claim it as yours before theirs glow? You keep that ticket at least for a while." He laughed darkly. "Like I said, a useful waste of a ticket."

"That's..." Tiffany shook in her seat as she looked at her lap. Joshua was shaken too. His ticket that was their get-out-of-jail-free card and now felt like three tons of weight laid in his pocket. His fingertips traced his pocket and felt the slick paper that laid inside. Now he understood why the woman said he should hold on to that ticket tightly. All the pieces fell into place for him. He might not know exactly how he got here yet, but he had a way out.

"Well, enough dark stuff for now!" Teff clapped his hands happily, and his smile brightened. "We need to move on to our next station." His hand grabbed a pocket watch from his pocket and checked the time. "We are almost late!" He gasped. "Well, late by my standard anyways." He raised his hand and rang the bell above his head. "Next stop! Hell! Floor one and the only station that they have in this layer!" Nobody moved. Everything still seemed too surreal to people as the engine roared with life. Joshua looked at his shoes with newfound interest. He searched his mind for any recollection of how he got here, but it evaded him. Panic thoughts swarmed his head as it felt like a bombshell was dropped in his lap.

He was dead, or near dead if that even mattered. His ticket was targeted the farther down that he went. It felt like a bucket of cold water had been dumped on him as the train slowly trailed forward. No random lurching, no fast speeds, only the agonizingly slow speed of the train. He gulped down dry saliva as he turned back to Tiffany. She seemed to be having a realization too by the way her eyes widened and hands clenched. He looked at Jason next and saw that the shock wore off. He sat back in his seat and found interest with the floor in front of him. *How the hell do you* not *care!* Joshua screamed in his head. He turned to Madeline next and saw the distraught written all over her face. It was not every day that you heard "You're dead" from a random train conductor. The mixture of distraught, anger, and disbelief was clear on everyone's faces as he surveyed the cart. Joshua turned back around and saw Teff stared right back at him as the train moved. His eyes were cold, and his smile was cryptic and unnerving. Joshua gulped down the bile in his throat and looked back out toward the window. Hopefully, this was a fast trip through hell and not an extended stay with a gift shop at the end.

Chapter 5

Hell City

THEY RODE ALONG AT an agonizingly slow rate for what felt like hours. Whether that was the case or not, no one knew. After what felt like the first hour, small chitchat started up again. Nothing nearly as cheerful as it was before. There was a sullen tone in their voices as their eyes begged to find out who had the near-deather ticket. Joshua did his best to keep to himself, but at the sound of Tiffany muttering under her breath, he turned to her almost immediately. They stared at each other for a long moment before either of them spoke.

"Do you know how you died?" Tiffany asked cautiously.

Joshua shook his head, and a frown cracked on his features. "Do you?"

"I think I have a pretty good idea." She hesitated.

"Really? W-well, if you don't mind me asking, how?" Tiffany stayed silent for a long moment, eyes focused on the wooden ground underneath her. He chewed on his lip as he waited on a response.

"I think I was beaten to death," she said at last.

Joshua gasped. "What?" he said a bit too loud. It got a few stares from the people around them, even Teff looked, but he settled down fast, and the stares died down. Tiffany nodded. "How?"

"I think it was where I was at last. I was seeing my boyfriend, and we were having such a nice time. But...he left me alone for a moment, and I was lured into an alleyway by whom I thought were his friends. And last thing I remember is getting slammed from behind in my head." Joshua covered his mouth at the cruelty. Tears stung Tiffany's eyes as she looked away.

Teff was beside her a moment later and knelt to her. He looked her in the eyes and had a soft smile on his face. "Do you want anything to forget for a while?" Teff asked. "It may not be permanent, but it is something."

Tiffany shook her head immediately. "No, thank you." He nodded and stood. He gave her one last look before he walked away and paid attention to the other passengers. After a minute, she glanced at Joshua. Her eyes were filled with dread and horror. The remembrance of her death was the biggest shock in the world to her. "Do you remember?" she asked quietly with a haunted expression.

"Huh?" Joshua straightened up a bit. His eyes concentrated on the seat in front of him as he searched his memories. Instead, his head stabbed him with pain. He curled in on himself as he gripped his hair. The pain throbbed and went from his head and spread throughout his body. Whatever happened, it was traumatic enough to leave the pain behind. He huffed as he heard his heartbeat through his eardrums.

"Joshua," he heard Tiffany say as he felt a hand on his back, "Stop thinking about it." Joshua breathed in heavily. His whole body convulsed, and he did his best to steady his breathing. The pain started to subside as he put his mind on a different topic entirely. He thought about the cars he and Tiffany talked about earlier. When the Ferrari spun into his mind, the pain died down bit by bit. He breathed in again and let go of his hair and laid back in his seat. He panted as he stared back at Tiffany. Her face showed her terror that reflected back to him. "Are you okay?" she asked.

"Never been better," he answered sarcastically.

"All right!" The sound of Teff's cheerful voice made a lot in the cart cringe. "Are we all ready for our next station?" Terror gripped Joshua's heart as he looked at the charismatic man. Joshua was not even positive if he could call Teff a man anymore. He gulped as he realized that he did not want to find out.

"W-where is our next station?" Madeline sheepishly asked.

"Well, we are going to our first hell station! It leads you directly into hell city! Satanica!" Teff chuckled as he glanced at the bell. "To be fair, out of all the stations, this one is the least terrifying. Outside of gang violence and territorial disputes, you really get off scot-free with demons only harassing you!"

"Only?" Jason asked incredulously.

"Compared to the rest, I'd consider yourself fairly lucky that some entity put you in such a good grace for being a complete scum." The graveness in Teff's tone as he stared down Jason caused the train to go deathly quiet. "Actually, after seeing your ticket, Mr. Jones, you should consider yourself *extremely* lucky. Because outside of a demonic vouching of the rules, you would be down in the last substation." His smile turned inhumane as he glared down the man. Jason sulked back into his seat and shook a bit. Teff reclaimed his usual smile after a minute. Joshua turned white alongside Jason. With a simple clap of his hand and a giggle, he grasped the bell and shook it happily. It rang in a sweet, songlike tone, and the train groaned as it came to a stop.

Joshua looked out to the seascape, and it was still. The waves stopped at its highest. Birds were paused midflight almost like he paused a movie. "Uh-oh," Joshua breathed out.

Suddenly, the train fell. All the people on the train except for Teff flew toward the ceiling as the force pressed against them. People screamed and cursed. Joshua took a glimpse at the window instead of the floor and saw flashes of dark red and pitch black that sped past. His heart raced. His mind clouded. He only prayed to some god that he had some medication after this. His nails clawed into the ceiling as they pressed on downward. With his peripheral vision, he saw Tiffany to his right as she screamed bloody murder and Madeline and Jason stunned to silence.

"Oh my god!" he distinctly heard someone shrilled out. Teff hummed amusedly at the statement, which caught Joshua's attention.

"God chose not to help you now," he stated quietly, but somehow it was the clearest thing Joshua heard from the whole train. Then everything stopped, and the lights went out. Joshua crashed onto the chair seats. His head collided with the back of the seat. An intense, familiar pain pulsed through his head. A groan escaped his lips and chorused with the rest of the cart. *God, why?* he asked himself. *I'd rather be anywhere else but here.* A heavy weight pinned against him that made it impossible for his body to move, a pressure that weighed down on his chest and legs more than anything. The cart felt hotter, and his lungs filled up with an invisible liquid the more he kept breathing. After a long moment, the sounds of footsteps drummed through his ears at a steady beat. Joshua's head pounded the familiar pain from the beginning of the ride. His head throbbed. He gritted his teeth as a picture in his mind formed. It was a blurry image. The scent of river water flooded his nose, and a deathlike chill now clung to his body. His lower half felt submerged in water. His fingertips felt the trickles of water that started to rush past him. A blaring loud noise overcame the footsteps that he heard, and the image barely started to become clearer with dark colors.

"Oh, no, no," he heard Teff say louder over the mirage that played before him. "You are not done yet." A hand clasped on his shoulder, and the air around him became breathable again. Joshua gasped in air, and the pounding of his head subsided into a dull ache. He immediately shot up and saw Teff's eyes stared back at him. He brought up a hand with a smile, and it was another blue pill. "Here, dry-swallow this." Joshua's eyes glared down at the pill and then back up at the man. His lungs began to hyperventilate as he stared between Teff and the pill. Teff grabbed his hand gently and slipped the pill in the palm of his hand. Joshua looked around. There was light again. There were brighter colors. The familiar scents of vanilla wafted back to his nose. The passengers groaned around them as few moved to get up. His attention turned back to Teff and stared at him in bewilderment.

"What is this?" Joshua asked between rapid breaths as he brought up the pill.

"Comfort for now," Teff responded. "Think of it like your medication."

"I—"

"Just take it for now," Teff interrupted quietly. Joshua took in a breath and dry-swallowed the pill. As the pill went through his system, the dull ache slowly slipped away. Teff nodded after he stared at Joshua for a few seconds. "You should take a look out the window. I'm sure you will see one hell of a view." Teff winked as he said it and stood. He walked away from Joshua and helped out the others on the ground.

Joshua got up and into his seat. The pressure was gone, and he felt lighter than a feather. He peered out the window. His gasp was caught in his throat at the sight. The city glowed from underneath them. It glowed a dark blood red, and the buildings looked no better than if they were from abandoned war zones. An explosion went off in the distance. A few others went off after that in different colors. There was black, purple, and white smoke that puffed into the air. He heard nothing, but it felt like he could. He saw boring yellow lights as they sped off through streets that he lost sight of against the rubble moments later. "A car?" Joshua asked a little over a mumble. "How are there cars in hell? How does that even make sense? What, did cars go here after they kicked the bucket?"

"What are you looking at?" Tiffany asked.

Joshua looked back at her and saw the distraught gaze. He nodded toward the window. "Satanica."

"Oh." She sat further into her seat.

"You don't want to see?" Joshua inquired. "There are cars here."

"Not really something anyone wants to see, Josh," she said sheepishly. Joshua nodded and looked back out to the view.

"Whoa," he heard Jason state in front of him as the man slouched back into his seat. "So that's home now I guess." Joshua looked over at his eyes as they lit up at the scene before him. Jason looked back at Joshua after a moment. "What?"

"Are you actually excited to go?" Joshua asked, stunned.

"Yeah," Jason said as he smirked.

"H-how?"

"Well, you don't know me, do ya?" Joshua shook his head. "Then you wouldn't get it."

"Well, how about explaining it?" Tiffany jabbed in. Jason shrugged as he sighed.

"Guess someone should know. Hell, I'm dead anyways. If one of y'all get that damned ticket to get outta here, tell my story, would ya?" he muttered as he turned toward them. Joshua slowly nodded alongside Tiffany. "I wasn't what you called an easy kid," he admitted. "I may have gotten into a bit too much trouble. Well, that trouble got me into a gang. But hey! It paid well, and I got protection from people that I screwed over. How could I go against it?"

"By, I don't know, going to college? Doing better for yourself?" Tiffany stated with annoyance. "You didn't have to be a bad kid."

"Check your facts," Jason said coolly. "I didn't finish high school. Got suspended too many times and my family wasn't paying for private school. Besides"—he shrugged—"can't say that it isn't cool to be a part of a gang." Jason chuckled as Tiffany rolled her eyes.

"So what, uh…ended you?" Joshua asked.

"Oh, I was shot by cops," he said with a wince. "Can't say that it was a pleasant way to go, but I knew that as soon as I ran it was either death or the big house." He relaxed back in his seat. "I was probably one of the first people that got to the station, and I had time to remember and think about my death. For where I'm going, Teff isn't wrong that I was lucky. I'm happy with it. I came to terms with it. I bet you there are people on here that still don't know how they died yet."

"You think they will find out?" Madeline spoke up. Jason looked over at her slouched back in her seat. "To be honest…I don't know why I died yet." She seemed very uncertain. "I don't know why I'm going to…wherever I'm going."

"Yeah, you'll find out," Jason said calmly.

"How do you know?" Joshua asked.

"Because it's a rule that even hell follows. The train conductors talked about it while they were walking the station earlier. These trains we're on are like different centuries and time zones, so they sometimes have time in between shipments of souls to talk and walk. I overheard that game Teff was talking about with the tickets long before we were supposed to board. I was able to do a switch out and get a way lighter sentence. Anyways, they have to tell the souls why they are there to give them that peace of mind to know where they belong. They were also talking about…I think they call it dimensional shifts? I'm guessing that's what we went through to get down here. I mean, did you see how everything around us just stopped?"

"No?" Tiffany questioned.

"I did," Joshua said quietly. "It was like a movie scene."

Jason pointed to Joshua to make his point. "See? I think physics and shit say that would be a dimensional shift."

"I mean…if Josh saw it too…" Tiffany said quietly. "Could be true then." Joshua smiled as blush dusted his cheeks. Jason nodded.

"Yeah, I think Teff will talk about it at some point probably."

"So you said you got a lighter sentence?" Joshua spoke up.

Jason nodded with an impish grin. "Hell yeah. Instead of where I was going, I ended up here! I call myself pretty lucky. Call it God or whoever saving me one last time." He shrugged his shoulders. "Some basic punk from like the 1920s kept staring around and figuring out where to go. I found the train, we traded the tickets, and he went on his merry way."

"So…where were you supposed to go if this is the lighter sentence?" Joshua inquired further.

"Yeah, this seems terrible, so where you were going had to be like a million times worse," Tiffany added in as she slid to the edge of her seat.

Jason's grin only grew wider. "For the crap I've done, I was headed to the end. The final station ticket literally says end on it in huge letters. I figured that was really fucking bad from what I was hearing from the other conductors."

"You would think that they would have kept better watch over the passengers and their tickets so that no one stole a heaven or purgatory ticket. Like security or something," Tiffany grumbled. "That's a total crap thing to do to someone that doesn't even know where they are."

Jason shrugged. "And I care becaaauuusssseee?"

Tiffany huffed and sat back in her seat. Joshua felt an anger inside him grow as he glanced back out into the cityscape below. This area looked horrible, but going further down would be worse if Jason was right. He gave Jason a hard glare as he looked back at him.

"Just because you started out with a shit life doesn't mean you can just shrug it off onto someone else. You had the chance to change it! You are the one that dropped out of school and went to a gang! You deserve that ticket, not stealing someone else's. That only makes you so much lower than the rest of us here. You *knew* where you were going and just said 'Fuck the next person' then," Joshua growled toward Jason.

Jason looked back at him, surprised, and then a glimmer of guilt passed across his face before a stone-cold glare took over. "Stay in your own lane. You're in the same hellhole as I am now, kid. People like me are not that uncommon, and you should know that if you're here too." The two growled at each other before they looked away.

Joshua tried to listen to the confused murmurs of the train as he calmed down. Some talked about death, while others wished for new lives. Tiffany shifted in her seat, and that caught Joshua's attention. He saw her look behind them into the other seats. Joshua turned around and saw a woman and man sat in those seats. Their hands were joined together in what looked like silent prayer. Joshua furrowed his brow. "Can God really hear you in hell?" Joshua asked himself.

"What are you two doing?" Tiffany asked. The couple finished their murmurs and then looked at the two young people. They stared at them for a moment before they responded. They looked between the two young people like they had grown extra heads.

"We are praying," the man said simply.

"But uh…why?" Tiffany asked, confused.

"Do you not know you are in hell yet or…?" Joshua asked alongside her.

"Because we don't feel we belong here," the woman stated calmly. She shuffled up in her seat and extended a hand to the two. "Hello, my name is Clarice."

Tiffany took the hand. "I'm Tiffany."

"Oh, but aren't you a boy?" Clarice asked, confused. Tiffany froze up and let go of the woman's hand. "Or are you one of those trans demons?"

"Trans demons?" Joshua asked defensively.

"People unlike the holy folk," the man said.

"Holy folk?" Jason called out from his seat. "Do you not realize where you are?"

"Oh, our tickets are screwed up, son," the man said plainly. "We have been asking Teff to get them fixed, but he says that he hasn't heard anything from management yet."

"I'm really about to ask for said management honestly," Clarice jibbed. Joshua and Tiffany looked at each other.

"Ignorance," Tiffany grumbled as she turned around. Joshua nodded with wide eyes as he turned with her. As he glanced at Tiffany, something in his heart tightened. He glared back at the jabbering nutcases behind him before he grumbled a few curses and turned back around again.

"You shouldn't listen to them," Madeline said quietly. Her eyes showed her hurt as she stared back at them. "You are a beautiful girl." The two stared at her wide-eyed for a moment before Madeline gave a sheepish look. "I heard them when they were talking to you guys. Thinking they could get out of here now is delusional at best. You are a beautiful girl though, and anyone can see that."

"So are you," Tiffany replied quietly.

The sound of hands clapping caused the four to turn toward the back of the cart. Teff opened the door and stood there with his usual smile, a smile that started to send horrifying chills throughout Joshua's whole body. "All right! Glowing tickets, anyone? We are now at station HL 1!" Jason pulled his ticket out of his pocket and waved it in the air along with quite a few others. They glowed like little fireflies against the light of the cart. At least half the cart alone was all the first level. Joshua stared at them in wonder. "Then line up and prepare to skydive! Anyone that needs new souls for their cults or gangs will grab you up from the city below!"

"Skydiving? All right!" Jason hopped out of his seat with a small kick to his step. "Seems like this is going to be fun." Teff was visibly irked as he saw the man saunter back toward him. People gave anxious glances to Teff before they decided to jump off. As the line went down, Joshua looked out the window in horror as people plummeted down to the city below. He saw as different winged black creatures took some souls from the sky. He cringed from the screams of pain that came with every one that was grabbed. The few that made it to the ground were out of his sight. He hoped deep down that they would somehow be okay. His attention glanced up as Jason was the last one in line. Teff stopped him, whispered something into his ear, and shoved the shocked man off toward hell city. Teff slammed the door with a satisfied chuckle.

"You can't outdo hell, everyone! Keep that in mind!" Teff exclaimed as he strutted to the front of the cart.

"Aren't we going to go through it and see it?" Madeline questioned.

"Would you want to?" Teff asked. They stared at each other for a moment. After a sigh, he leaned up against Madeline's seat dramatically. "This level of hell is only the first of a whole journey through the rest for some of you. Why would I let you all see the relaxed version that you all will inevitably wish for? Even I am not that cruel to set something in front of your face when you have no chance. If you all do it to yourselves though, that is up to you. Like hoping for heaven in the midst of hell." Madeline's eyes lost their shine as Teff pushed off her seat. "Just know I do this for your bit of sanity left, not my own." His smirk was sad and sinister at the same time. "Right," he said with a clap, "off we go then!" He strolled up to the bell and rang it louder than normal. "Besides, the station is so broken and irritatingly smelly! I hate going there if I don't have to." The train trailed in midair again. "Next stop! The second level!" Teff cackled as the train started moving at a rapid-fire speed. "Oh, and hold on tight! Might be a bumpy ride! Turbulence sucks down here!"

Chapter 6

Time to Shift!

THEY GO THROUGH THE sky with Satanica far off in the distance. Joshua's anxiety caused his heart to beat through his ears as they left. They did not fall like they did on earth. Nobody spoke. Everyone sat in an uncomfortable silence. Joshua tried to breathe in and out quietly, but everything seemed enhanced to him. He breathed too loud. Everyone heard his heartbeat. He swore there were eyes on him as he gazed out the window. His fears raced through his head. He thought that in death there was supposed to be peace. Apparently not. In the middle of darkness, all he had were his thoughts. That was a hell that he admitted to himself he never wanted. In fact, in life, he did absolutely anything and everything to keep his mind away from it. Hours upon hours of video games, social media, and mindless entertainment. Now his life and problems were shoved in his face with all this time. It seemed like a cruel ending to his life in his mind. Suddenly, something caught his eye that brought him out of his darkening thoughts. A huge spirally blue ring came to life before his eyes. "What is that?" he muttered quietly.

The train started to turn and head straight for the spiral. He looked up and saw Teff look around the cart from his little spot in the front of the aisle. A content look fell on his face as he looked over his patrons. When Teff felt a pair of eyes on him, he turned toward Joshua and gleamed with happy curiosity. "Can I help you?" he asked happily.

Joshua was taken aback by how fast he was noticed but opened his mouth and pointed to the spiral outside. "What is that?" he asked curiously.

Teff leaned forward and looked out Madeline's window. "Oh! That's the dimensional shift! Nothing special."

"Dimensional shift?"

"Yeah," he said with a nod. "A dimensional shift. You mean you don't know what that is?" Joshua shook his head in response. "Tch, tch, poor school systems teach nothing these days," he hummed as he stood in thought for a moment. After a second, he snapped his fingers and walked over to Joshua and motioned him to stand with a wave of his hand. "I don't do this often, but stand, my friend, and join me up here. I'll show you what I mean." Joshua gulped down his hesitation as he did so. "Anyone else want to know? Take a stroll along the train?" No one moved. As Joshua glanced back at everyone, he saw a mixture of fear, pity, and sadness in the crowd. In fact, no one seemed to even notice that Teff said anything at all. "Hm, rude," Teff huffed. Joshua did not comment as he shuffled past Tiffany. She looked even more deep in thought than the rest. He waved a hand in her face when he moved into the aisle, and she did not flinch.

"Don't worry about her," Teff said quietly. "She is doing what everyone else is when they are near a dimensional shift. They reflect."

"Why are they doing that?"

Teff started to walk down the aisle slowly and monitored the passengers as he went. Joshua followed behind closely. He witnessed hopeless faces and different moods that swung through the faces he passed. "Why do any of us reflect? Because we are realizing what we are doing wrong or right. In their case, they are seeing their sins and responding to it properly." Teff shifted his hat as they got to the back of the train. "These dimensional shifts are also shifting energies. Perception takes up energy wavelengths to the brain just like any other thought process. Near dimensional shifts, that energy is stronger, so a person is more willing to look back on their lives with keener perception. It doesn't work on everyone though. Some brains are able to block it out until they are at closer range. You, for example, pulled yourself out of it or never went into that reflective state of mind."

"So…where are we going?" Joshua asked. Teff did not respond; instead, he tapped against the wall of the back of the train. The wall moved up slowly and revealed a door. The door was tall and made with black metal like the outside of the train. It had a small window that showed the different carts behind them, carts that Joshua forgot even existed.

"We are going up, dear boy. And don't worry about breathing. You don't really need it." Teff opened the door and walked out onto a small platform on the back of the cart. Joshua stepped out, and air immediately left his lungs. It was like he was sucked into a void, and his lungs shriveled up like a balloon. He gasped and coughed and felt as if he was drowning. "Stop breathing," Teff suggested calmly. Joshua shut his mouth and, after a long moment, felt his body open up. It was like he was lighter after a moment. He nodded to Teff that he was okay when the conductor raised a brow. "Now don't speak. You will want to breathe if you speak," Teff stated. "Just follow me and listen." Joshua nodded. "Up we go!" Teff hummed as he grabbed on to a ladder that was drilled into the exterior of the train. He hopped onto the ladder and started to climb.

Joshua followed slowly behind him. He held on to the steel with a deathlike grip. As he climbed, he realized that nothing pushed against him. No wind. No inertia. Nothing. Teff got on top of the train with ease and helped the boy up next with a smile. Joshua looked out into the distance and saw the spiral slowly became bigger. It also seemed to him like they traveled faster from this viewpoint on top of the train compared to when they were inside. *Were we really going this fast the whole time?* he asked himself.

"All right, now," Teff started as he turned Joshua around at the other carts, "do you see these carts?" Joshua nodded. He marveled at the size of this train. The carts went back for miles. "Now you see how there are so many of them, but they only make up one train?" Joshua nodded again. "Now let's think of hell as a train. There are carts that are the actual levels and substations that hell offers us to stop at to drop off souls." He leaned the two of them forward and pointed to the doors and then to the connection between the two. "Those would be your dimensional shifts. You're moving from cart to cart until you get to the very front." He then turned them to the front of the train and stared at the steam engine. "And when you get to the front, some crash, while others get off unscathed. You'll know which one you are when you get over there." He smiled toward Joshua. "You are never going further down in hell. You are already at the bottom, and the only way to go is from left to right." Joshua stared off at the spiral that they steadily grew closer to. "Do you understand?" Joshua nodded. "Rather simple, isn't it?" He nodded again. "The most interesting thing is that sometimes most things are that simple and no one wants to admit it." Teff chuckled. He continued them forward toward the steam engine up front.

Joshua wondered where they were going, but he saw that Teff aimed straight for the steam engine. They walked to the front of the cart, and Teff took in a long breath. Joshua raised his brow as he witnessed Teff stare off at the spiral. He saw a mixture of grief and distraught on the other's face, a look that he never thought he would witness.

"You know, you near deathers should be taking this all as gospel," Teff said lowly. "You all actually see what the process of death may come to. Your ticket even tells you, if you were to die, where you would go. Purgatory if no demon or angel questioned it." He chuckled sadly. "A second chance. Something I see millions now beg for no matter where they go." Teff sat down. "Come and join me, Joshua." He motioned him with a pat on the metal next to him that made no noise. Joshua sat down and felt the bone-chilling cold of the metal. He shivered a bit but became used to it quickly. "You know, I really like watching from up here the dimensional shift. Well, from the first to second level. For some reason, the energies get even stronger the more we go through them. Sometimes, at the final one, it even gets me to think back on my past life." He chuckled for a moment. "That was almost a hundred years ago."

Joshua's eyes widened. Teff was...old. Very old. He looked so young. Joshua had so many questions yet could not ask any. He wondered if that was the real reason he sent the two of them up here: so that he could not comment. Teff stared out into the distance and no longer commented to Joshua. Joshua's attention turned back to the spiral that came closer and closer. He saw, as the spiral came closer, that there were little balls of light that circled in and out of the spiral. Some had streams of white and purple that faded in and out of it beautifully. It looked like a galaxy that turned into a black hole. He shifted a bit so that he could see above the steam engine and watched as the head of it went through. Balls of lights splashed out around them, and there was a coolness against Joshua's body as their cart entered. Balls of light shifted around them that were no bigger than snowflakes. Joshua stuck his hand out and touched one. It vibrated in his palm and immediately let it go. Teff chuckled.

As they went through the hole, they came out onto the other side, and it seemed like they were in an entirely different world. Joshua scrunched up his nose in confusion. It was a nice neighborhood. It had the charm of a suburban home with an average lawn and garden with bright-blue cars in the driveway. Every house looked exactly like the other. Different people were in plain gray suits and glasses that Joshua had not seen except for in a fifties TV movie. In fact, now that he thought about it, this looked like a neighborhood from the 1950s. He glanced back over at Teff and heard the sigh and contempt that overcame his features.

"I hate this substation." Teff motioned with his head over to an average-looking bus stop. "Always so dull to look at, isn't it?" Joshua nodded. Teff shook his head as he sighed again. "Welp, better get the next batch ready. They will have some adjusting to do." He stood up and motioned for Joshua to do the same. They headed back toward the other end of the cart slowly. Joshua glanced back for only a second before he followed Teff down the ladder. "Oh, and by the way," Teff said as he held on to the door outside of the cart, "you should watch more closely on who is around you. They are not as innocent as they appear to be." Teff smiled sadly. "Just a word of caution. You're already lucky that some soul like Jason didn't find *you* at the station."

Chapter 7

Never Enough...

THE MOMENT THEY WENT back through the door, Teff knocked and hid it back behind the wall. He motioned Joshua with the wave of his hand to go back to his seat as he glanced out the exit door. Joshua complied and walked down the aisle. Confusion filled his head as he walked. Teff could not mean Tiffany. She was so nice in Joshua's eyes. Madeline? No, she was too hotheaded but a nice person to him. Joshua gulped. He got stared down by the other passengers as he walked over. When he opened his mouth, he stumbled a bit as air gasped into his lungs. Air flooded inside him like a tidal wave. The sweet feeling of air and working lungs was enough that it brought the boy to tears as he trailed up to Tiffany's gaze. "And where were you?" she inquired cheekily. "Are you turning into the conductor's pet or something?"

Joshua shook his head. "Trust me, you don't want to go where we went. It was...breathtaking."

Tiffany stared at him. After a moment of thought, she nodded and moved so that he could squeeze in. "Where are we now anyways?" Tiffany asked.

"Another substation," Joshua answered.

Tiffany peered out Joshua's window before she scrunched up her nose. "Just looks like a bus stop in a nice neighborhood to me," she commented. "What's so awful about that?"

"Right? I wouldn't mind this version of hell at all from how it looks," Madeline added as she turned to her traveling mates. "I wonder what is so wrong with this one."

The sound of the door opening had everyone jump in their seats as they looked toward Teff at the back of the train. Teff said nothing as he let in people in dark gray suits with Einstein-worthy glasses. Joshua shrunk back into his seat. What was going on here? The men worked silently as they went through the rows. When they stopped at a person with a glowing ticket, they forced the person out of their seat and held on to them viciously. When one of them got to their row, they stared at the three with a blank stare. Its eyes were black and voided of life. They all stared at one another for a long moment before Teff stepped in. He shoved the thing back and hissed at it. "If they don't have a ticket, then move along." The threatening hiss from Teff was returned with a scowl, but it kept moving. Teff scowled back, and it quickened its step. "Talk about pushy…," he grumbled lowly. "HL 2A! Glowing tickets for HL 2A! This is your station!" Teff called aloud.

"I don't understand. What is so bad about here?" Tiffany asked rather loudly toward Teff. Before Teff could respond, the demon that stared at them craned its head. It whipped its head in a complete 180 from its body and glared at Tiffany. The hunger in its eyes was evident as it stalked backward to her. Teff stood in the way and hissed again. That stopped the thing, and it stood where it was. A smile crossed its face. Sharpened teeth on a humane-looking smile nearly stopped Joshua's heart.

"When you crave to have so so sssooooo much," it said in twisted, high-pitched squeal, "this is *heeelllll!*" Tiffany shuddered back into her seat, which caused all the gray-suited things on the train to laugh. They all had sickly high-pitched shrieks as laughter and inhumane smiles. Everyone on the train cowered away, and the people they held struggled against them. Glowing tickets clutched tight in their hands as they squirmed. One woman struggled so much that the thing snapped her head so that it was upside down on her head. The woman screamed in agony as she squeezed her eyes shut. Joshua's stomach dropped to his groin and dry-heaved.

"Get off the train!" Teff shouted. "I will talk to your management if I am late for the next substation!" Teff seethed as the things straightened up at the threat. They were quick to take their people and get off. Teff took out his pocket watch and stared down at the device. A sigh of frustration escaped his lips as the watch slipped back into his pocket. "We may be late," he grumbled again. "I hate this substation. I want to beat my best times. How am I going to do that when they are so theatrical?" He stalked to the back of the train. His eyes skimmed the seats as he did so. When he was sufficed with what he saw, he slammed the door shut after another hiss escaped his lips. His feet stormed back up the aisle and hands rang the bell angrily. "Off to the next substation," he spat. "And good riddance." They sped off from the station as the train erupted to life. As Joshua watched the sight before him start to fade, his eyes caught the people that were left behind. They were shoved and forced into the same exact clothes as the rest of them.

"I changed my mind about this hell," Madeline squeaked as she curled in her seat and looked toward the ground. They chugged along the road to the next substation as tension filled everyone in the room. Joshua kept himself on the lookout for any of those things to follow. Relief filled him when nothing did. As they got farther and farther down the neighborhood, it started to change. The homes were not as nice as the ones from earlier. They looked almost worn down and abandoned, yet people in tattered clothes loitered around them. Some of the people looked broken and mistreated. For being in hell, they seemed sadder than tortured. The pictures of torture that Joshua saw in books and movies were nothing like this. They all looked downtrodden, and some even glanced toward the train in hope. It pulled at his heart as they rolled by. The train did not give a care in the world of the souls or demons outside of it.

They ended up in a part of the neighborhood where the houses were not houses. Instead, they were cardboard boxes on the sides of broken-down roads. The people inside were dirty and grimy. Some cardboards were built higher than others, but overall, they all had their clothes hung outside and firepits were in the center of some cardboard circles. No one looked fed. Joshua found someone that drank water from a dirty puddle near some garbage cans. This looked like some form of hell to Joshua unlike the other part. They screeched to a stop, and Teff walked to the back of the train. Everyone watched as he opened the door again.

"Anyone with a glowing ticket?" Teff asked. "We are looking for HL 2B! HL 2B, everyone! 2B!"

"No!" said a man that Joshua found spoke a bit too earnestly. Teff cocked his head to one side as he looked over the man. He was a large middle-aged white male with wrinkles all over his face. His eyes looked hollow and his hair receded and graying.

"Well, that was enthusiastic," Teff commented as a demented smile fell upon his face. "And I am sure you would not mind showing me your ticket again if that is the case?" Joshua stared at the man. The man crouched back into his seat and held on to it tightly. It was clutched too tightly in the man's deathlike grip.

"I have no reason to show you anything!" the man stated too loud.

"But I'm the one in charge," Teff explained, "so you *must* show me." The man shook his head and shut his eyes tight. He seemed terrified. His nails clawed into the seat like a scared cat. Teff slowly crept up to the man and glared at him. His smile turned cold and cruel as he leaned down over the woman that sat next to him and stared at the man. "Show me your ticket, sir?" Teff asked with a calming chill to his voice. "I would rather you show me while I'm happy. You won't like me when I am not happy." The man opened his eyes, and Joshua could not see Teff's face. But the look the man gave proved enough to Joshua that he did not want to see Teff's face. The man stiffened, and his face turned wan with fear as he reached into his pocket and pulled out a glowing ticket. Teff snatched the ticket from him and straightened back up. He flipped the ticket to the back and cleared his throat as he started to strut forward on the cart.

"W-what are you doing?" the man choked out. Joshua noticed the front of the ticket. It had a huge HL on the ticket and 2B neatly on the corner of it.

Teff's eyes skimmed something on the back of the ticket and chuckled to himself until he reached the front of the cart. "Hollander

Duggery," Teff said humorously. "A fancy name for a man," Teff chided. "Forty-five years old, has one kid that he never claimed, and died of a stress-induced heart attack from overworking and the classic American diet of cheeseburgers and fries." Teff started to slowly stroll back down the aisle. "Your greed preludes you. You are such a money-grabbing muck that you disowned your child at birth, never took responsibility for the thousands of people you put out of work because it saved you three hundred thousand dollars, and ran company after company into the ground. You paid your way to the top and tore down every competitor in your field. That and you sneered at everyone that you came in contact with that wouldn't sleep with you. It even said that on some accounts, you forced yourselves upon them." Teff leaned against the woman's seat that sat next to Hollander and looked him dead in the eyes.

"I-I never did any of those things."

"Tickets don't lie," Teff replied matter-of-factly. "And from what I read, this is the perfect form of hell for money-grabbers like you that don't have the decency to care for other human life. In a hell where you will never go up from being a beggar and never have the chance to succeed." Teff moved and motioned for Hollander to get up by the crook of his finger. "You can either leave willingly or I can get the demons of this substation to come and grab you. Either way, this is your stop on the train."

"This is unfair!" the man shouted out angrily as he stomped his foot on the ground.

"And you had a whole lifetime to change it," Teff stated knowingly. The man grew silent. "You are dead, dear sir. There is no changing that now. Now maybe you can repent and possibly get into heaven, but even that is rare to see. But your time is up, and so is your train ride." Teff smiled coolly. "Just think, at least it was great with the living and you saved a few bucks, right?"

The man shook his head and refused to leave his seat. "You are horrible," the woman next to him commented toward Hollander. Hollander stared at her, wide-eyed.

Teff's eyes rolled upward and turned away from him. "I'll get the demons," he sighed dramatically as he trotted toward the door.

He leaned out of the doorway, and Joshua saw him as he waved his arm in the air. "Come and get him!" he hollered out. A few of the homeless-looking men got up. Their eyes glowed a deep color of gold and had dirt smudged on their faces. They had ragged clothes on, and their hair was long and greasy. They stared hard at the train as they walked up. There were at least a few dozen that moved up to the broken-down area they parked at from what Joshua counted. Joshua shuttered a bit. They did not look thin but looked starved.

Demons, he assumed thoughtfully.

"Now, now, now. There is only one!" Teff exclaimed as he let two of them on.

They were tall and towered over the people that sat on the train. They stared down at everyone with hard, hungry eyes. They were not like the other ones. These ones stood motionless in the center of the cart. They turned their heads inhumanely back to Teff. Their necks cracked and snapped as they did so, and Joshua winced. Teff said nothing and motioned his head toward the man in his seat. The demons said nothing but turned their heads a full three hundred and sixty degrees. Then they stalked up to the man and waited for him patiently. The wait was scarier to Joshua than if they had just grabbed the man and dragged him off. Joshua clawed at his seat as the demons stood there patiently and stared. The man shuffled anxiously in their seat. No one moved. No one spoke. They only waited patiently for the man to get up.

After a long silence, the man got up with his head hung low. Tension dissipated as he left his seat. Whether it was due to peer pressure or awkwardness, Joshua was not sure, yet he was glad that he went willingly in the end. The two followed him off the train pressed against his back. Teff nodded to the demons before he shut the door as they walked out. Teff sighed loudly as he walked toward the front of the train. Tiffany and Joshua jumped toward the window and watched the man with interest. Their eyes could not look away. The longer they stared, the weaker the man seemed to be. He turned pale, and his face wrinkled and scrunched together in pain. His clothes became worn down and torn apart. When he looked frail and elderly, the demons let him go to the rest around a group fire.

The sound of the bell tore their eyes away. Teff did not pay anyone mind as the train crawled away. They started off at a slow pace, and it rapidly increased the farther they went.

Teff clapped his hands. "All right! Now our next stop is to the next level of hell! Time for part three!" He smiled sweetly and leaned against the wall.

Joshua glanced over to Tiffany as she sat back down in her seat. "Wonderful," she commented sarcastically under her breath. Joshua shrugged.

Chapter 8

The Tar Pits

JOSHUA FELT REMINISCENT AS they neared closer to another dimensional portal. He succumbed to the warmth of memory that came to his mind. He was back in school. Just another average day. His fingers tapped on his wooden desk and heard the teacher as she droned on and on, on a topic that he could not for the life of him remember. Something prickled toward the back of his neck. It was not fear per se. More like a warning. Something that he had always hated about himself. The way the hairs on his neck stood on end meant that someone stared at him. As he sat there, he tried his best to ignore the eyes that were on him. He looked down at the papers sprawled on his desk. They must have been unimportant because the writing was fuzzy along with the pencil.

The bell rang, and his eyes looked up. He saw Mrs. Parker, his high school precalc teacher, as she returned to her desk to help other faceless students. But the thought of where he was alarmed him. He knew where he was and who stared at him from behind. He shot up from his seat as he looked down at his old band T-shirt and ripped-up blue jeans. His heart dropped into his stomach. He was quick and ran out of the room. His feet guided him through this memory as his heart pounded. His lungs started to hyperventilate. He found himself in a cornered area of lockers. His locker sat in the middle of it all like a beacon of light that called to him. *All I need is my coat and keys, and I can leave,* he thought with a little bit of hope that this was a different memory.

"Joshie boy!" A hand slammed on the locker next to his head, and Joshua jumped.

Aw, crap, Joshua whined in his head.

"D-Darren," Joshua stuttered as his anxiety got to his voice. The boy with the dark-blue eyes and darker brown hair gave Joshua a shark-tooth grin. Someone leaned up against the locker behind him. Joshua shut his eyes. He remembered that there were two people behind him: Joey and Connor, the two biggest people on the football team. He opened his eyes as he looked at the current quarterback.

"You want to know what makes me upset, Joshie?" Darren asked as he leaned against the lockers and crossed his arms. Joshua shook his head as he winced at the stupid nickname. "You didn't produce last night."

"I told you I was *not* giving you the homework. Do your own work!" Joshua hissed.

A chuckle erupted from Darren's throat. "Well, if you were serious," Darren said as he snapped his fingers. An arm went around Joshua's mouth as the other went around his arms and waist. With Joshua's small frame, he thrashed and struggled to no avail. Darren tightened his fist and punched him in the center of his chest. The wind was knocked out of him, and he was let go. His body fell onto his knees, and another punch swung into the side of his jaw. His head slammed into the locker and felt a foot dug into his chest. His body knocked back into the legs of the guys behind him.

Why the hell are there no kids around here yet? Joshua asked himself before memory served him an answer. Nobody came. Nobody showed up in this hallway that day to help him. His memory reminded him how the other football players blocked off this corner. They were a barricade that no other high schooler would dare cross. Another swift punch knocked against his chin. The locker screamed for him as the side of his head banged against it. "Damn it," Joshua cursed lowly to himself.

Darren crouched down and grabbed Joshua roughly by his shirt. "Now," Darren said almost sweetly as his lips curled into that shark-tooth grin, "what were you saying about my homework?"

Joshua gulped. His body groaned as it felt the swelling around his jaw and the pounding of his head. A metallic taste trickled into his mouth, and he almost reflexively gagged. "It'll get done," Joshua groaned in defeat.

Darren patted his shoulder hard and shoved Joshua's body into the lockers before he stood. "Good, good. I'll expect it tonight. Same time, right?" Darren asked. Joshua numbly nodded and rested his head against the cool metal of the gray locker. All three of the men stepped back and walked away from him. Joshua stayed down there as air refilled his lungs and the new throbs of pain chorused throughout his body.

"That was a rough one today." Joshua grimaced as he wiped away some blood that trickled down his lips with his hand as he stood. He shook his head and turned back to his locker. "Fucking hate this life. I wish it would just all end. Go away and never have to come back," Joshua mumbled to himself as rage and depression filled his chest.

As the locker opened, something similar to ice shocked him back onto the train. He jumped in his chair as his eyes shot open and looked around the cart. Other people silently murmured or glanced around, but nothing happened. Nothing touched him that reminded him of ice. His eyes glanced over at Tiffany and saw that she was lulled in her thoughts. When he looked up to Madeline, she was caught up in a conversation with a charming boy from across the aisle. His head turned around and saw the couple as they prayed again. Teff stood in the back of the cart and conversed with another group of people. They showed him their tickets and seemed intrigued with what Teff had to say. Joshua shook his head and rubbed his eyes. He felt dazed, almost as if he came out of a drug-induced sleep.

He turned his head and peered out the window as he had been doing this whole trip. This time, the area was painted in varied shades of gray. It was void of color, and loss of hope filled his heart as he gazed out. Small mounds of gray separated different swirling black pits. The pits bubbled and steamed. Joshua pressed his nose up against the window as he stared in awe. A lone substation up ahead among the gray wasteland stood cracked and broken. A frown cracked across his lips. It was no better than a gray box with a lighter gray sign with Substation imprinted on it in black ink. The train rolled up to it and came to a soft stop. His attention caused him to turn around and look toward where Teff clapped.

"Anyone with a ticket?" Teff called aloud. "Look for your glowing ticket! We are at HL 3A! We are at HL 3A!"

Joshua searched around. Two people stood. His eyes looked back to Tiffany and saw her dazed expression. His fingertips lightly brushed the woman, and she sprung to life. Her expressive eyes stared at Joshua with a wild stare. "Are you okay?" Joshua asked cautiously.

Tiffany shook her head as she rubbed away the glassy expression from her eye. "Y-yeah," she said quietly after a moment. Her hand jutted in her pocket and took out her ticket. It glowed the sparkly white hue, and Joshua caught the gasp in his throat.

"No…" Joshua said, pained.

Tiffany shrugged. "It's my stop."

Joshua bit his lower lip. When she stood, he grabbed her arm and forced her back down. "I thought you had the other ticket!" Joshua hissed to her.

She raised her brow to him as a confused expression fell on her face. "What are you talking about?"

"The near-deather ticket. Teff said there were two. I thought…I thought you would have had it. You're so nice. You don't deserve to be here! I just…I just assumed that it wouldn't be you leaving this train."

"Josh, it's fine. I know why I'm here, and I'm not fighting it. I deserve it."

Something filled his heart, but he could not identify the emotion. He clenched his teeth together for a moment and swallowed it down. He shook his head. "No, you don't." He grabbed the ticket from his own pocket and shoved it in her hand and took hers without thought. He stood from his seat and waved the ticket. "I have mine," he said calmly.

"Joshua, what are you—" Tiffany tried to talk him down.

"Look at the ticket," Joshua stated quietly as he moved from his seat. He showed Teff the ticket, and Teff stared at him in bewilderment. They shared a long look before his eyes went to Joshua's companion. Teff sighed but took the ticket.

"This way," Teff said quietly as he stepped aside. Joshua gulped as he moved his way into the aisle and made his way out. He stood at the exit door that he entered in the very beginning and saw the box of a substation. His heart dropped to his stomach. He took a final deep breath of vanilla and stepped off the train. The door shut behind him with a distinct click. An immediate weight from the atmosphere around him made it hard to breathe but bearable enough.

"You weren't strong enough" whispered into his ear. He looked behind him and saw nothing but the steam engine. He shook his head and took a couple steps forward. "You wanted to be more than this. A real woman." Joshua's back straightened as he walked away from the substation. "Why did you do it? Why did you choose to die?"

"Choose?" Joshua asked out loud. *But Tiffany said that she was killed by getting pummeled to death,* Joshua thought.

"It was never from the beating you got from haters. It was what happened afterward. Don't you remember the rope?" The whisper echoed in his head. Rope? Realization hit him like a brick wall. "You remember." The whisper in his ear caused him to look for a source. Instead, air released from the train and slowly started to chug away. He gulped down his rising fear and turned back around. His feet guided him to a pit. His eyes concentrated at the black substance as it bubbled and stewed. A sweet scent, however, wafted to his nose. An inviting presence of the pit overcame his thoughts. He stepped forward and into the tar. It felt like a heartbeat swirled around his foot. When he tried to pull it out, it clung to him. The warmth caused the muscles in his foot to relax, which made it harder as he pulled. After a moment, that warmth crept up his leg, and an overwhelming sense of home overcame his senses. He took a deep breath and plunged further in.

A scene unfolded before his eyes as if it were a misty dream. He saw Tiffany crying. She was beaten and bloodied. Her makeup was smudged as tears fell from her eyes. Joshua tried to stick his hand out toward her but to no avail. Her watery eyes never glanced at him. He noticed her dress was torn and hair was disheveled. Joshua felt tears pricked at his eyes as he watched. A protectiveness swelled in his chest as he saw her curled up on the ground. His fists tightened as Tiffany stood. In full sight, she really did look like she was a beautiful girl outside of this moment. She was stunning and looked even more feminine than how he met her. He opened his mouth and tried to speak, but nothing came from his throat. All he could do was watch helplessly as Tiffany walked out of his sight with a broken heel. The area turned into pitch darkness around him.

Another scene faded in before his eyes. Tiffany was sobbing as she tied a rope into a noose. Joshua forced himself to move forward, but his feet were glued in place. Frustration filled him. *How useless can I be? Why can't I help her?* he asked himself in full frustration.

"So I'm not girly enough, huh?" He heard venom from Tiffany's usually sweet voice as she spat blood on the ground. "A freak? A disgrace? Doesn't anyone want to even *see* my point of view?" Tiffany shook her head as tears continued to fall. Rage seethed around her as Joshua nodded. Joshua tried to voice his answer, but his lips were sealed together. "No…the answer is always no." He watched helplessly as she took the noose and walked away from him again. The familiar darkness fell down around him.

A third scene surrounded him. He saw Tiffany with the rope around her neck and stood on a small chair. He shook his head. Terror shook him as he saw the emotionless glare in her eye that seemed to pierce through him. Her outfit changed to a small dress, and her face was painted on. She looked gorgeous, but traces of bruises were still evident. A cold fury flickered in her eyes, and that nearly stopped Joshua's heart. "A freak, huh?" Tiffany asked that to herself. "Maybe not in the next life." Joshua tried to push himself forward before Tiffany did anything. However, his efforts were cut short by a hand that grabbed his shoulder. It pulled him out from his knee-deep trap before he witnessed anything further. He gasped as the gray world came to view around him again. He spun and hit the ground hard with a loud thud. Tears flooded his eyes as he saw Tiffany and Teff. He got up from the ground with lightning speed and hugged Tiffany tightly.

"Please, please, *please* don't do it! Tell me you didn't do it!" Joshua sobbed openly as tears stung his eyes. "You didn't deserve it!"

"Josh…" Tiffany did not finish as she held on to him. They held each other tightly.

"We can go back and be friends! I'll be there for you! Tiffany, no one will hurt you anymore." Joshua cried. He wiped his tears away furiously as he stood a foot away from Tiffany. Her eyes shone with unshed tears as she stared at him. She bit her lower lip. "You never deserved it…," he choked out quietly. The next hand he felt on his shoulders was Teff's. He turned his attention to the conductor and then saw the train that sat at the station behind him. Why did they come back?

"Joshua," Tiffany said quietly with pain in her voice. "If we could turn back the clock and meet in life, everything would be different. But it's not, and this is not the sacrifice you are supposed to be making for me."

"Joshua," Teff interrupted as he held out a dull ticket with PP written on it.

"B-but I gave her my ticket," he said quietly.

"And I am giving it back," Tiffany said just as quietly. Joshua stared between the two of them.

Teff slid the ticket back in Joshua's pants pocket. "Joshua, what you have to understand is something that almost no one does. This is her stop." Joshua gritted his teeth. "And I can promise you that, unlike most, she will be in good hands." He motioned to the pit behind them. "Depression is a tricky topic and has caused a lot of accidental deaths throughout time. Accidental deaths, or better known as unjudged deaths, are sent here until they are sent through another judgment. And I pick those souls back up and send them where they properly go, which may even be back in purgatory to restart a new life. A better one typically. Think of this as hell's version of a waiting room." Teff cracked a small smile. "You know how

Christians say all suicides go to hell? This is where they get it from. But I promise you, unlike what they think, she will be rejudged and sent into better hands. With her age and track record that I read, she will definitely be in better hands."

Joshua's jaw slacked. "B-but I just had to—" Joshua started.

"Endure the worst part for her," Teff interrupted him. "These pits are no better than comfort zones. Depending on the watcher, it can be pleasant or not. And for her, I promise you, it will." They looked back at Tiffany. She nodded.

"I did this to myself, Josh. Don't…don't take this for me. Who knows? I may even see you in the next life?"

Joshua frowned.

"This isn't your fate, Joshua," Teff said a bit more sternly, "And she was the one that stopped the train to make sure I knew that she wanted to take her place." Joshua's gaze fell on Tiffany, and she nodded in agreement. He gritted his teeth in defiance but nodded and stepped aside. Teff took ahold of Joshua's arm and nodded for Tiffany to the pit with his head.

"I'm sure you will be put into the right hands," Teff said softly to her. "You seem to be a wonderful person to me. I'm surprised you didn't get heaven immediately."

"Thank you, Teff," Tiffany said quietly. "And thank you, Josh." Joshua nodded with a sorrowful look.

"I'm sorry, Tiffany. You never deserved that."

"No one ever does," Tiffany said quietly. "Maybe when you go back to the living, you can spread that message for me." Joshua nodded, and something inside his chest burned with pride. The goal entered his mind that he would do anything to spread Tiffany's message. "Tiffany Watson is the name you are going to Google-search." He nodded, and determination filled his eyes. They watched as Tiffany went over to the pit and lightly dipped her feet in. When she was submerged in the pit, Teff forced Joshua back toward the train.

"You need to watch your back now," Teff stated gravely as they made their way back toward the opened door.

"What do you mean?" Joshua asked.

"Everyone found out that *you* have a near-deather ticket." Teff nodded toward the cart entrance. "Get back on the train."

Joshua gulped in fear. He crept onto the train, and all eyes focused on him. Some were hungry, while others were cool and calculated. Teff followed behind him, and they all turned away. A familiar fear crawled up Joshua's spine. The hairs on his neck stood. He was being stared at again. As if the memories earlier were not enough, now he was being glared down by the whole train. He crawled back into his seat and sat as close as he could to the window. His throat wanted to close up as he stared out the window. He gazed directly at Tiffany's pit as if she would crawl out at any moment and get back on the train. Sadly, the click of the door pricked his ears as it shut, and Teff strolled up the aisle. He did not clap his hands. No smile was on his face. He grabbed the bell and rang it loudly, which signaled the train to start back up. His hand grabbed for his pocket watch and cursed to himself. Joshua assumed that they were all late to the next station, and it was because of him. He took in a shaky breath as the train headed out of the station. And off they were, on another adventure, farther into the pits of hell.

Chapter 9

Anxiety Overdrive

BEING IN A POOR community sucked, especially for his family. They could never afford much, but they usually made do with what they had. He remembered that most nights would be sat in front of a television and stared at a lit blue screen. Some random person yelled at them through the monitor, and it always captivated his little sister. She wanted to be a movie actress so badly. And seeing how she always lit up a stage in her school plays, it was not that outstretched a theory. The last thing he would want Sophie to do was worry. She was always the worrier of the family. *A talent that she had gotten from Mom.* At least, he thought it was from their mom. He never saw her enough as a kid to make that assumption. She was always so busy with work or doing her extra schooling so she could get a better job. She was supposed to graduate by the time he started college. Dad loved her idea of getting a degree and better pay. That way, he could cut down hours at the car shop, at least temporarily. Joshua remembered hearing his dad cry some nights when he got back extremely late from work. It would end up with him wishing he could cut hours or find easier employment so he would not have to be up again in five hours to start another workday. Sometimes his mom would hear him; other times, only the bottles of beer he drank did.

He always had alcohol. It helped him fall asleep easier, especially recently. Hearing that he might get laid off from work made the man work that much harder to prove his usefulness there. In Joshua's eyes, he was the hardest-working man that car shop owned. And if they did not want him, Joshua would think best that he left and go somewhere where they did appreciate him.

"Poor Dad, I should have told him to quit," Joshua muttered under his breath, his eyes glazed with his thoughts. Joshua realized after a moment that they had not hit another dimensional shift. In fact, all they did was get plunged into total darkness outside. He saw nothing except his own reflection in the window. He saw the curly dark hair and fear-filled eyes. He looked like the usual train wreck he was in school, just with better clothes. He sighed as his head laid against the cold glass.

"Hey." The meek voice pricked at his ears. His attention turned to Madeline as she peeked over the seat to him. "Want some company?"

He stared at her for a moment, then shrugged. The ticket was in his pocket near the window. To not notice her hand there would be a failure worthy of losing his ticket in his mind. Madeline stood, and Joshua noticed the thinness of her again. He frowned. *She looks thinner and thinner the more I notice,* he thought.

She sat down next to him and sighed. "Man, this has been one scary ride. Don't you think?" Madeline asked in a shaky voice.

"Yeah," he said lowly. He turned to face her and saw the hurt in her eyes.

"Look, I don't care if you're a quiet kid or what ticket you have. Don't need to sound like a jerk and not give me more than one-word responses," she spat.

Joshua smirked. Her spitfire personality grew on him. He sat up a bit straighter and nodded. "Sorry, you're right."

"So was it scary out there?" she asked.

"Terrifying," he admitted.

"Looked it." She looked past him and out the window. "This… is more intimidating though. I don't know how the driver can see where he's going." Joshua glanced out the window and agreed. "Do you think Jason would have been scared?" Joshua perked at the question as he turned back to her. Blush crept on her cheeks as she looked away. "Never mind," she grumbled.

"I think he would have been. I mean, I admit that I don't like the guy that well. Or really…ever will."

Madeline held back a comment as she sunk into her seat. "Yeah…that's true," she mumbled.

"Sorry," Joshua said quietly as he realized he hit a soft spot that she must have had for him.

"No need to be," she commented back quickly. He was ready to say something back before a loud bang against the glass had him jump into her lap. She held on to him, and they both stared bewildered at the window. The darkness was all that stared back at him. "What in the living hell was that?" Madeline squeaked just barely above a whisper. They looked at each other, stared at Joshua on her lap, and then back in their eyes. He jumped off her and back into his own seat. She blushed furiously alongside him.

"It was, uh, the sound," he barely managed to get out through his embarrassment.

"Right, the noise," she replied.

"What even was that?" Joshua asked. Suddenly, he was answered with more bangs against different windows and walls on the cart. His heart leaped into his throat. People around the cart gasped and screamed at the sounds. Joshua felt his chest tighten as he pushed himself to the very edge closest to Madeline.

"What the hell?" They heard the couple behind them shriek. Joshua grabbed at the heart that beat out of his chest. This was his hell. He barely breathed because everything felt too sudden and randomized around him. His fingers clutched at the edges of his seat with angst. He took in deep breaths and tried to think of cars, girls, anything to get his mind off the problems that went on around him. God, this anxiety reminded him of when he was home. Back where problems surged around him left and right.

"Oh, thank God it stopped," Madeline breathed fearfully. Joshua shook himself out of his anxious daze as if suddenly aware of his surroundings. The banging stopped, and everyone on the train was in a panic. The tension that laced the air was so thick that it could be cut with his dull pocketknife.

"God, I wish I was home," he said as the tension died down in his chest.

"Same! I haven't stopped thinking about it since we got on here." She shook her head and looked at the back of the seat in front of her. "It seems so surreal, knowing that you're dead. You know, I thought we turned into ghosts and could scare the living shit out of people for eternity, but this...this is downright terrifying." She shook her head sadly. "One day, I'm worrying about what my calorie count is for the day and I'm trending on my social media, and now...now I...I don't know why I was even worrying in the first place." Her eyes looked down to her hands, and Joshua noticed the skin that clung to her bones. "All I wanted was to be beautiful while I was alive. Ha, that sounds so stupid now."

"But you are beautiful," Joshua stated earnestly. "Even if you didn't see it, you are. I can see it plain as day."

A small smile fell on Madeline's face as she turned to him. "I wish someone would have told me that before I became so hell-bent on it. It's all I ever wanted to believe." Joshua nodded slowly. A pang of regret for Madeline fell upon his heart.

She must have gone through a lot of hell in her own mind before getting to this point, Joshua commented quietly to himself. He opened his arms to her, and she silently stared at him. "You look like you could use a hug. My little sister always told me that when you see a sad girl, you offer a hug."

Madeline chuckled, and it sounded sad and distraught to him. But she fell into his arms and accepted the embrace. "I wish I had known you while I was alive," Madeline said shyly.

"Same here," Joshua admitted. "Maybe all of us would not have been here if we did." He let go of her, and they shared a smile.

"Well, we have met now, and I think we could be cool friends," she said as hope laced her tone. Joshua agreed with a nod.

"So tell me about yourself. I'm assuming you're a social media star."

"Yeah, kinda," she said with a small chuckle as she scratched her red hair. "My social media name is Red Star. You know, because of the hair?" Joshua perked up to the name.

"Hey! I know that name," he said happily. "Sophie follows you!"

"Sophie?"

"My little sis." Madeline turned grim as he continued. "She loves your content. Raves about you all the time. I wonder why I didn't notice you before this! You're like her idol." His eyes looked around on the train before he gulped. "Well…was her idol."

"I should never have been," she replied, her face turning more serious. "She should never have followed anyone like me."

"What, why?"

"Have you even seen my content?"

"I mean…a little. You post good selfies." His cheeks blushed as the words blurted out.

"No, I mean the actual posts." Joshua shook his head. "You should pay a bit more attention to the platform. Josh…I… I am not a role model. At least, now I'm really seeing more of that the more I'm reflecting on this train." Joshua furrowed his brow in confusion. A groan of frustration came from her as she rolled her eyes. "Well… girls follow me because of the diets that I do," she motioned to her body as a reference. "They follow me so that they can lose weight and be practically skin and bones like me. It's not healthy. I literally hashtag paper-thin as my thing."

Joshua's eyes widened. It did start to make sense in his mind. Sophie had been skipping dinners the past few weeks from his memory. And breakfast. In fact, how often did she eat real meals anymore? She did also look a bit thinner, but he never said anything because he was not sure how she was doing it. His eyes trailed over Madeline while the pieces came to place in his mind. An anger kindled within him, but he could not tell if it was at her or at himself. "So she's… she is bringing herself to possibly…being the next person in here," he stated grimly.

"Not if you stop her, she won't." Madeline bit her lower lip.

"She was losing weight and skipping a few meals, but…I never thought about it. She only started this a few months ago."

"I'm so sorry," Madeline apologized.

"Why would you promote that?" Joshua snapped at her. The anger swelled inside his chest. "That sounds so dangerous!"

Embarrassment flooded Madeline's features as her face reddened darker. Joshua saw the reaction, and immediately his anger calmed down into sorrow. He took in a deep breath and relaxed back into his seat. "I'm sorry, I—"

"I was made fun a lot," Madeline interrupted as her face turned deeper shades of red and winced. "A lot. I was known as Fatty Maddie when I was younger. I…guess you could say I was chubby." Her eyes trailed her body and frowned. "People stared at me. I was always told there were cheeseburgers on the ground, and sometimes they even threw snack bags at me." Her eyes grazed her hands specifically and shuddered. "I…I was taken to fat camp one summer after a particularly bad accident at school. Kids shoved different pictures of pigs in my locker with a stuffed animal with my name written in Sharpie on it. And then at the end of the summer, it was like I was a brand-new person. I—" The sounds of banging picked back up again, which cut her off. Joshua looked out the window, still the ominous darkness that loomed over them.

The train started to slow down as the banging picked up. It pushed the train as they rolled slower and slower. The train swayed bit by bit with every hit. Joshua braved himself toward the window and looked out and saw a lit-up yellow station. It cast a bright halo-like glow around the outskirts of the small station. It looked no different from a bus stop in the middle of a woods. A horror scene in Joshua's mind. The woods that the light shined upon was a sight that had Joshua pressed against the window to see. It was a dark forest with a sea of trees that cascaded everywhere. In fact, there was no way of seeing past the first row of trees. The whole area was cast into an eternal midnight with no moon or stars in the sky. A clapping of hands snapped Joshua away from the window. Teff stood with his usual charming yet sinister smile as he walked toward the back of the cart.

"Anyone with a glowing ticket getting off here?" he asked out loud. "The ticket will have HL 3B on it! 3B!" He opened the door.

Everything became silent. The banging from outside immediately stopped. A tension fell upon the cart. Whatever demons were here were Joshua's worst fears. His anxiety gripped him tightly. He glanced over to Madeline. She stared at the seat in front of her. She found some interest in the material that it was made of as she refused to look anywhere else. He saw nothing glowed on her. His head turned around and paid attention to the other people on the train. A small man that looked terrified out of his boots shakily brought up a ticket with his right hand. His dark skin gleamed against the glow of the ticket, and his thick-lensed eyes stared wildly around him. A sweat broke out on his head as he got onto shaky legs. He walked into the aisle and stared at Teff with deerlike eyes. After a split second, he darted off toward the front of the cart. Teff rolled his eyes as he peered out the opened door. The man aimed for the door in the front and banged on it wildly.

"Lemme out! Lemme me get reincarnated!" It came out as a high-pitched squeal, and Joshua winced internally. The pleas crawled through his head as the door banging drummed in his ears.

"We got a runner going at the purgatory door!" Teff called out of the door. The man stopped banging wildly at the door and stared back at Teff.

Everything was quiet for a moment. Bangs hit at every side of the train like randomized chaos in a split second. People gasped and screamed as the train shook and tipped from side to side again. A loud, unearthly shriek ripped through Joshua's ears. He clutched his ears as his eyes squeezed shut. Once the noise stopped, he opened his eyes yet kept hold of his ears. A mixture of pure fear and agony froze him in place as he saw his worst nightmare in the middle of the aisle. A monster so tall that it hunched over as it was in the cart. It looked like a skeleton covered in slick black skin. It had holes for eyes and a gaping mouth with razor-sharp teeth. Spikes came out of its body in different directions and sizes. The man at the purgatory doors stood stark straight in fear. The monster looked at him. In the blink of an eye, it stood right next to the man. Joshua's hands went from his ears and rubbed his eyes to look again.

"What the hell…" Joshua stated under his breath. Faster than anything he had ever seen, it towered over the small frame of the man underneath it. Joshua's heart dropped as it unhinged its jaw. Joshua immediately gripped at his seat as his heart leaped to his throat.

Razor-sharp teeth poked out of the jaw, and the man shrieked. Then the thing let out a high-pitched shrill. Joshua felt his own life flashed before his eyes as he stared horrified at the thing in front of him. The man matched its scream. It grabbed the man by the neck and threw him to the other side of the cart. Joshua looked back and saw a claw-like hand of an identical creature grabbed the thin man and pulled him all the way out. Joshua took in deep breaths. *Oh no, oh no, oh no. Please tell me this is over!* Joshua prayed in his head. As Joshua turned around to sit in his seat, he became paralyzed. The thing's face was only inches away from his own. Fear stopped his heart, at least he thought it did. Soulless black eyes stared back at him. Neither moved. It slowly brought up a slick, spikey hand and pointed at him with a long, lanky finger. The tip of it touched the top of his fore-head. It felt no different from a chunk of ice touching him.

"Yoouuuuuuu are next," it growled in a whisper-like voice. Joshua gulped as he chose to remain paralyzed with fear.

"Hey, he doesn't have a glowing ticket," Teff snarked as he walked over to the two nonchalantly. "Get off the train. He was the only one." The demon stared up at Teff. Teff's glare chilled Joshua more than the demon did. With a small nod, it stood up and towered over Joshua.

"Nexxxxt time," the thing said as it glanced back at Joshua and then stomped off the train.

"Hopefully not," Joshua squeaked out of himself. The things disappeared into the night. Wherever that man went, no one saw him from the train. Joshua did not bother to look too hard either. He was frozen in place. He heard the door slammed shut. His eyes stayed on Teff as he strolled back over to the bell and rang it, a chime that sung so sweetly in Joshua's ears. His heart did not calm down until the train was in motion. Once he saw the dimensional portal in the far-off distance, he felt his chest lightened up slightly.

"What was that all about?" Madeline asked as she leaned over to him.

He shivered. "I don't ever want to find out."

Chapter 10

Seduction Is an Art!

JOSHUA RELAXED BACK IN his seat as he watched them get closer to the portal. His eyes glanced over at Madeline as she remained glued to her seat and eyes focused on the back of the seat in front of her. He nudged her with his elbow, and wide eyes stared back at him. "So what were you saying before we stopped?" he asked.

Her eyes averted away from him. "Nothing," she muttered coldly.

"C'mon," he started. "You were bullied, sent to fat camp, and then what happened?" She remained silent. Joshua took in a deep breath. "If it helps, I was bullied too." Madeline's body stiffened. Her head snapped back to him. He nodded. "Not hard to believe, right? I was the nerd at my school. The jocks beat me up if I wouldn't do their homework. You know, it sucked getting my ass kicked all the time, and I was the loner. I didn't have friends, and girls think I'm a weirdo because I'm always drawing comics in my spare time." He pushed up the jacket of his right forearm and showed her something that got him grounded for months after his sixteenth birthday. "I got a tattoo of my own comic hero when I turned sixteen. Friend of mine's cousin did it cheap." She giggled when she saw the tattoo of a superhero emblem from a character of his very own design. An old-school recording microphone with an A in the middle of it was inked in the middle of his forearm. Pride shined across Joshua's face at both his confidence and the drawing that laid forever on his arm.

"You draw?" A small smile grew on her face as she asked.

"Yeah," he said as faint red dusted his cheeks. "I know, I know, laugh it up."

"I find it cool," she admitted. "And those bullies were probably dickheads in all honesty." He agreed.

"So you willing to tell me what happened after fat camp yet?"

She shrugged and sighed as her body relaxed back in her seat. Her shoulders sagged. Her eyes were tired as she looked around. She bumped her head on the back of her seat and stared at the ceiling. Joshua turned to her fully and leaned sideways against his seat. "I was popular as soon as I got back to school. They thought I was even a new kid at school." Her eyes closed in remembrance as she spoke. "No more Fatty Maddie. No more food getting thrown at me. Just… attention and friends and boyfriends. And well…I didn't want other girls to go through what I had to. So I became an influencer." She opened her eyes and shook her head sadly. "And I guess I thought I was doing something right, but I'm quickly realizing that I was wrong. And it made my eating disorder worse. I was diagnosed with anorexia a few months ago, and a lot of people said that social media wasn't helping my case. But…I thought I was helping others. Giving them a guide to a thinner, healthier life. I guess not."

Joshua frowned deeply. "I mean that doesn't seem…inherently bad actually," he admitted quietly. His eyes looked up toward Teff and saw the feminine man as he watched over them. Silver eyes stared at them, intrigued, as if he were listening to a story. Teff turned away when he realized he was spotted and walked down the aisle. Joshua's brow quirked, and his attention went back to Madeline.

"I don't know," Madeline admitted. Her tone was lost and gentle, which worried Joshua more.

"In my mind, she could have lost a few more pounds," a female's voice muttered behind them. Madeline shrunk in her seat. Joshua glared at the couple behind them. The woman averted her gaze, while the man coughed and looked out the window. Joshua's anger bubbled up inside him. The two seemed unbothered by his gaze. He turned around slowly and grumbled to himself.

"Ignore them," Madeline said quietly after a long moment. "That isn't the first time I've ever heard that."

"But they're wrong," Joshua growled under his breath. "You are perfect the way you are. No one should have made fun of you to begin with." His head shook bitterly. "I don't understand any of this," he spat quietly after a moment. "Sure, some people had real reasons to be here, but you and Tiffany...I just don't understand."

"Tiffany was a special case," Teff said from beside the two. Madeline and Joshua jumped from their seats as they turned to him. He swirled around and took the seats in front of them. Teff smiled to the two. "I explained to you that where you got off was no different from hell's version of a waiting room. And she will be rejudged."

"Wait, what? Why?" Madeline asked.

"There are cases that even shock the supernatural," Teff admitted after a moment. "Suicide being one of them. When someone dies before they are due, there is no fair way to judge them at first, so they have to go into waiting. While in the living realm, everyone views the real purgatory as a waiting room when that just isn't true. The tar pits are what they are actually referring to. It isn't hellish like the rest of these dimensions, which have obvious reasons for a soul to be there. They shocked the system and need to sit and wait. Typically, suicide victims outside of cults, and even then there are moments where the members are drugged unfairly, are unexpected and are lost souls that were so unfairly treated that they felt there was no other way. Typically, it is a last resort for anyone, not the first." Teff looked toward Joshua after the explanation, and a frown tugged at his lips for only a split second before he returned to the conversation. "Homicides are another type where souls could end up there. However, those are rarer."

"How are those rare?" Joshua asked curiously.

"Because in some way or form, they usually align with fate," Teff explained matter-of-factly. "A sad but true reality. It is rare to see someone purposefully killed without a purpose, and typically those that are killed without purpose are usually good people and end up in heaven through mercy. Just like that little girl that got off in the very beginning."

Their eyes widened. "She was murdered?" Shock plagued Madeline's face.

"How else do you think she got on here? A bus?" Teff asked. They turned quiet in thought.

I forgot about her, Joshua admitted to himself.

"How…how did she get on here?" Joshua asked anxiously.

Teff dug a hand into his pocket and pulled out the tickets. They no longer glowed. In fact, they were a dull-gray color. He skimmed through the tickets as if he were looking through a set of cards in his hand. He plucked one out with two fingers and put the rest away. His eyes glanced over the back of the ticket, and a frown fell upon his face. A sad sigh escaped his lips as his head shook with grief. "She was stolen and sold in a human trafficking ring," he mumbled just barely loud enough for the two's ears. "She was bought and killed after she refused to provide service for a patron." Teff frowned deeper. His eyes skimmed more but remained silent. After a moment, he slid the ticket gently into a separate pocket. "Sad, isn't it? The way some die?"

They nodded. "Sad and wrong," Joshua commented. Teff agreed.

"Teff, why does it happen this way?" Madeline asked.

Teff perked at the question but was at a loss for an answer. After a moment, he shrugged. "I couldn't tell you," he said solemnly. "That is higher up than my payroll dictates." The two did not comment further but nodded. After a moment, Joshua noticed the small sparks of the dimensional portal swirled from outside. As they started to go through, he felt his head throbbed just a bit. A dull ache this time. His head rested on the back of the seat, and he closed his eyes.

"Joshua, please…" His head pounded worse as his ears strained to hear that whispered into his right ear.

"Sophie?" he asked out loud. The pain in his head grew, and his brow furrowed. His face twisted in pain. A foggy, blurred picture took place in his mind.

The scent of water hit his nostrils. Wind rushed past his ears. The air was cold against his skin. It looked like he stood above a huge bluish-gray mass with green that bled into the edges. His head gazed down toward his feet. He stood on something that was a dark brown. He had his regular old, raggedy shoes on that had holes in them. He also saw his faded jeans. There was something next to him. It was small and black. A sudden huge pang of pain on the side of his head and shocked him out of his thoughts. His eyes shot open, and he gasped in air as he held his head.

"Joshua? Are you okay?" Madeline asked worriedly as she placed a hand on his arm.

He looked over at her as his hard breathing subsided back into rhythm in his lungs. "F-Fine," he uttered out.

"You know, if you need to talk…" Her voice trailed off as her eyes flashed to the window. "What in the hell?" she asked aloud.

Joshua turned and viewed out the window. It perplexed him as he shifted closer. "This is a dimension in hell?" he asked to no one in particular. Murmurs of the train fluttered in his ears, but he could not decipher what anyone said in particular. His eyes scanned the area around him. They were in a hallway, to what Joshua recalled, no different from a hotel. Cream-colored walls holding different abstract paintings surrounded them, a plush red carpeted floor was beneath them, and the doors staggered as the hallway continued. Joshua's window stood in front of a door with 2650 written in gold at the very top.

The sound of a hand clap had Joshua jump out of his skin. His head whipped around and was met with Madeline as she chuckled. They both turned around and saw Teff's usual smile as he clapped again for everyone's attention. Once all eyes were on him, he proceeded with glee. "Who has a glowing ticket for the fourth level! We are at station HL 4!" he sang out.

Eyes searched the train, and three people brought up their tickets. Confusion laced their faces as they peered out windows and slowly stood. Joshua noticed a girl no older than twenty with purple hair, an older white man with a faded hairline, and a petite Asian woman that looked like a saint with her hair pinned in a neat bun and a stoic expression on her face. They stepped toward the aisle, and Joshua noticed how empty the cart was. There was less than half of the people from when he started. Then again, a lot of them got off either in heaven or the first level of hell. Few seemed to get off in the other levels thus far. *But there was still an undetermined amount of levels to still go through,* Joshua thought. His attention turned back to the people as they trailed off toward the end the cart. His eyes stayed trained on them, curious to know what demons controlled this area.

Teff's hand went up when they reached him and gathered their tickets. He motioned them back with his ticket-filled hand, and they stepped back awkwardly as he stuffed the tickets in his pocket. "This level is a bit different from other levels," Teff stated as he shooed them back until they were stuck in a huddle in the middle of the aisle. "They will choose whom they play with." Joshua's brow arched in curiosity. Teff went toward the door and opened it. "Your play-mates are here!" he called out. He chuckled amusedly as he turned back into the train. Snickers hissed from people that remained seated, while the ones that stood turned cherry red. Doors swung open from farther down the hallway as his eyes drew back to the window.

This was not something entirely too horrifying in his eyes. The things that came out were not terrifying to look at. Instead, it was quite the opposite. They were beautiful, gorgeous, and overall cap-tivated him. They all wore some form of skimpy leather outfit and, one even had a bullwhip. Their eyes sparkled and shimmered like glitter. A few of them exited their rooms, five in total, and sauntered toward the train. Teff stepped aside and averted his eyes as they passed him. One brushed up against him seductively, and his body stiffened. Three of them were women, while the other two were men. A dude with a six-pack and tight leather shorts walked around the two ladies with judging eyes. He locked his gaze in on the small Asian woman and stepped up to her. When she looked at him, her eyes glowed. It was the same shade of dark green like his, and her body leaned into him. He took her into a muscular arm and held her close with a dark smirk. His dark, tanned skin seemed to captivate the girl as she stared at it in awe. Joshua cocked his head. The arm tightened around her as Joshua looked up and saw the possessive gaze from the man glared back at him. Joshua's eyes snapped away from the two and watched as the other four strutted around the other two potential candidates.

One woman with fiery red hair and dark-golden eyes gave the purple-haired girl a once-over. The woman responded with a flirtatious wink and pushed some strands of violet hair from her face. The woman snapped her fingers, and the purple-haired girl had her hands strapped together with leather cuffs. The purple-haired woman's eyes glowed and then turned into dark gold, which matched her counterpart. When Joshua caught the eyes of the other woman, he noticed she had the same colored eyes, and a predatory grin graced her face. The woman grabbed the cuffed girl and led her out of the cart. The other eagerly followed behind, and the buff man with his lady walked slowly out after them. The other man-like demon seemed to thoroughly assess the middle-aged man. The older man looked back disgusted as concentrated eyes rolled down his body.

While they stared each other down, the woman with the whip looked further on the train. Her long blond hair flowed down against her thighs. Her breasts, Joshua realized, rivaled the size of watermelons. Her bright-blue eyes scanned around the train as if she could pick from any of them. Her gaze settled down on Madeline, and a smile spread across her lips. She and the woman stared each other down for a long, tense moment. After a minute, the woman strutted over and sat on her lap like she owned Madeline. Joshua pushed himself back until his back was against the window and watched. The woman grabbed her whip and wrapped it around Madeline's neck. She tugged the girl forward until their faces were mere inches away from each other. "You look like fun. You want to come with me?" she asked playfully. Madeline squeaked and shook in her seat. The woman slowly constricted the whip around her neck, and Madeline gasped in response. Out of fear or arousal, Joshua was not sure. "You would be fun to groom into a succubus." The woman gazed into Madeline's eyes intently. He noticed that her eyes flashed back. The whip was unwrapped from her neck, and the woman stood up. The dark mark stayed around Madeline's neck like a choker. Madeline tried to stand, but the woman placed a booted foot on her lap, which made her stay. "Stay put, kitten." Madeline's body shuddered and nodded eagerly. The woman flashed a seductive smile toward her before she turned away. Joshua's eyes scanned over Madeline as the woman strutted away. Madeline's eyes trailed after her longingly.

"Madeline?" Joshua called to her lowly. Her attention only watched after the woman with the whip. Joshua followed the gaze and saw that it stayed on the woman as she motioned Teff with a crook of her finger. The conductor relented, indifferent to the woman's charm. They spoke in a hushed whisper that Joshua could not hear. His attention turned back and saw the older man as his eyes glowed the same dark red like the demon he was with. His head cuddled in his shoulder as the gorgeous man held him tight. He walked over to the woman and Teff. The two moved aside, and they made their exit. The last woman scrunched up her face in hostility as she spoke to Teff. After a moment of debate, they both walked over to where Madeline and Joshua sat. Teff stared between Madeline's eyes and the woman's.

"See? She responded to me," the woman replied as she lightly caressed Madeline's face. The girl purred in response. "You know the rules, Teff. If they respond, I can take them and turn them into my own. Does not matter what level they are meant for. We need more succubi. There is a shortage after all."

"My words are final. If you want her, grab her from the level she is dropped off at. It's a fair trade at that point with whatever demon is supposed to be tormenting her," Teff argued. "And it leaves me out of it." The woman grunted in frustration as she rolled her eyes. "Or you could just wait for the next train and choose from that pack of sinners. I'm sure that conductor would oblige you."

She shook her head. "I have been down here for millennia, Teff. And I know what I want." She leveled Teff with a glare before she turned back and petted Madeline on the head fondly. "I want this one." Her gaze stared affectionately down at the girl. "She's just my type."

"I didn't know succubi had a type for slaves," Teff muttered.

"Show me your ticket, kitten," the woman said seductively to Madeline as she ignored Teff's comment. Madeline fished out her ticket from a pocket and handed it to the woman. The woman's eyes scanned over the ticket and nodded as she handed it back. "I'll be back for you," she said quietly. Madeline whimpered almost like an animal, but the woman only chuckled as she took a step back. "Stay."

Madeline watched her obediently as she was escorted to the back of the cart by Teff. Teff nodded to her as she slowly walked out of the cart. Once she was off, he sighed in relief as his eyes went heavenward. Madeline whimpered as the door shut. Joshua gently turned Madeline around and was greeted with a blank stare. He snapped a finger in her face, but she did not flinch. In fact, she was no better than a mannequin in his mind.

"Madeline?" Joshua questioned.

"Please tell me that was all the tickets," Teff called aloud with irritation in his voice. When no one responded, he took the silence as his answer and raced to the front of the cart. Joshua went back to Madeline and waved in her face.

"Madeline, come on. If you want to date a demon, cool, but come back to reality here!" Joshua exclaimed as he snapped a finger in her face. The bell rang clear a moment later and snapped her out of her trance-like state. Her head snapped to the train conductor, and her eyes flickered back to their normal color. She shook her head as the train slowly chugged forward. Joshua looked out the window and saw the woman that stared at their window as they left. Annoyance laced her face. Joshua shrugged and turned his attention back to Madeline. "Hey, are you okay?" Joshua asked.

Madeline stared back at him, perplexed. "Yeah, why wouldn't I be?" she asked back.

Joshua's mouth gaped open. "B-but that woman…?" He motioned back to the hallway as it passed by.

"Yeah, I know. Weird, right?" Her brows furrowed. "I don't know why she kept staring at me, but hey, whatever." She shrugged it off and relaxed back into her seat. Joshua closed his mouth and stared at her in shock. But after a minute of silent contemplation, his shoulders shrugged and eyes looked away. The train moved forward, and all he saw were closed-room doors that passed by. He sighed internally as he watched the doors turn into blurs as the train sped up. As they moved, his eyes caught on the image from the window behind him. The couple stared at Madeline intently and then shuffled closer together. Whispers came to his ears but nothing discernable, and they shifted their gazes from her back to each other. Joshua gritted his teeth as he watched them silently.

What problem could they possibly have? They are in hell too! Joshua growled to himself. After a moment, the comment of them going to management came to memory. *Of all things, they deserve to be here.*

"So, Josh," Madeline spoke up. Joshua pulled his gaze away and turned back to Madeline. "What's your sister like? If she was a follower, I'd love to know something about her." Joshua perked up at the thought of his little sister and nodded.

"Sophie is honestly the biggest drama queen in the world," he started. "You see, she absolutely loves theater." As he talked about his sister, he heard a whisper or two behind him every once in a while. Joshua felt the anger that slowly raised his blood pressure but took in a deep breath. *They'll get what they deserve sooner or later,* he thought.

Chapter 11

When Is It Too Much?

JOSHUA AND MADELINE LAUGHED at an old story about Sophie as the train chugged along. Small interjections from the peanut gallery behind them made them irk in irritation from time to time. Joshua grew in annoyance but kept to himself. Madeline ignored them with casual flicks of her hair toward them. The dimensional portal laid in front of them in the distance. As they made their way to the edge of the dimensional balls of light, Joshua irked as he heard yet another comment that escaped from the woman behind him.

"Sounds like they really were pieces of work, huh?" The woman chuckled as the words escaped her lips. Joshua's teeth clenched together from the tension that came from unsaid words.

"Hey, cut them a break. They're young," the man uttered back quietly.

"Yeah, but look where they ended up," the woman replied with a subtle scoff.

Joshua breathed in roughly through his nose as his reflection turned to the window. His eyes glanced to the window behind him and saw their gazes on their backs. A smirk cracked on his lips as he noticed their ears perked as they leaned forward. His heart pounded in protest of what came to his mind, but his head was so sick of the comments that he ignored it for once as he turned to Madeline. "Hey, Madeline?" Joshua nudged her with his elbow. She hummed in response as she turned to him. "You know something cool about this train?" he asked her.

Her brow raised in curiosity and turned herself more toward him. Her eyes glanced sideways as they felt eyes on them. She gulped as she gave her attention back to Joshua. "What's up?"

"You know, it really shows how some people are just judgmental pricks." He lowered his voice as he leaned in closer toward her. "Especially the selfish pricks that sit behind us." Madeline cackled as they went through the dimensional shift. The people behind him scoffed, and his attention turned to the horrified gazes that he got in response.

"Excuse you, young man, but that was completely uncalled for!" the woman exclaimed outrageously.

"Oh yeah?" Joshua asked with a raised brow.

"Of course!" she stated back. "It's untoward of anyone to do!"

"And what do you call your peanut gallery commentary this whole fucking train ride?" Joshua snapped back. The woman visibly shrunk in her seat as her faced turned pale.

"Don't you have any respect for the people older than you?" the man snapped back at Joshua.

"Only to people that deserve it. Not insensitive pricks like you," Joshua growled back. The man opened his mouth to comment, but his eyes flickered upward and clamped his mouth shut. Joshua glanced back and saw Teff's glare pointed at the group of them from the front two seats that he leaned against. A predatory smile fell upon his face as he caught their attention.

"Excuse my intrusion," he said politely as venom laced his tone. "Please do not fight on my cart. If you want to argue, take it outside at your stops." Joshua's heart fell to the floor as the color left his face. He nodded shamefully, and his eyes darted to the floor. "Good." Teff said it cheerfully. Footsteps drummed in Joshua's ears as Teff walked by them. Joshua huffed from his nose as a gentle elbow nudged at his arm. He glanced over at Madeline. He caught her wink and sly smile, which he returned before his attention went back to the window.

His eyes were met with a view that he had never thought was a reality before. "Whoa," he commented as his forehead pressed against the glass. It was candy land brought to life. Lollipops were as high and wide as treetops. Gumdrops laced sugary graham-cracker roads. Chocolate flowed out of small fountains. A river flowed nearby the red licorice train tracks that they rode on. It fizzed, and Joshua heard the crackling of soda through the window. He licked his lips without thought as his eyes traced cupcakes that popped up from the ground like flowers.

"Talk about Willy Wonka setting up his chocolate factory," Madeline chided as she peered over Joshua's shoulder at the view.

"Isn't it cool?" Joshua asked as his attention turned toward her. "I was always a huge fan of the movie. I mean, how can you not wanna see that factory in real life?"

Madeline responded with a half shrug and nonchalant hum. "Never really appealed to me honestly," she admitted. "Then again, I was always into horror movies myself."

"That makes so much sense," the woman behind them commented.

Madeline whipped her head and glared at the woman. "What the hell is your problem?" Madeline growled toward the woman. "You have been nothing but a judgmental prick this whole time. You know, you are here too! You are stuck in the hell sector with the rest of us! Don't pretend that you are above it all when you clearly are not!"

The woman scowled at Madeline. "I told you that it was a mistake with management," the woman snarled back.

"By the way you're acting, obviously it's not," Madeline bit back.

Joshua glanced around the cart as the two fought. His eyes fell upon Teff's as the man stared at the two women. Joshua's throat clogged up as the train conductor shifted his body, so his direct attention fell upon the two. "Oh, shit," the man behind Joshua cursed lowly. Joshua's heart leaped to his throat as Teff slowly inched forward. The conductor's eyes concentrated on them like they were targets to a sniper. Joshua shrunk against the window as his anxiety tightened his chest. Joshua's eyes averted back to the two women that growled at each other like feral cats. He moved his hand to touch Madeline's shoulder, but anxiety flooded his mind and brought his hand back to his side. Teff crept up to the two without either noticing. He waited for a moment and watched as the two interacted. Joshua thought he saw the thoughts that went through Teff's head as the conductor's light eyes drifted from one to the other and back. He felt the train as it slowly came to a stop. Teff did not move, and the girls did not notice. After a moment, a tired sigh escaped Teff's lips, which caught the girls' attention. They snapped their heads up to him, and their faces drained of color.

"You know, I swear I make the simplest rules for souls to follow. In fact, they are typically so simple they needn't be said most times." Teff sighed again and leaned against Madeline's chair. "Don't pick on others, don't masturbate while on board, no fighting. Such simple rules, yet somehow they end up broken." He dramatically rolled his eyes toward the sky. "Why does a god make such incompetent people sometimes? I'll never understand, and I've been dealing with them for a hundred years now!" He stared back down at the two and then toward the other men that sat behind them. "Since all of you cannot get along, all four of you will be moved to sit next to the few passengers that are still here." Teff motioned to the rest of the cart with his hand.

Joshua's head snapped toward them. Six people outside of them remained. Joshua's eyes scanned the rows of empty seats that once held passengers. It brought an oddly chilling silence in his heart. *Wow…we are missing a lot of people,* he thought.

"Wait, why are you moving me?" the man spoke up.

"Guilty by association!" Teff smiled as he moved aside. "Now while others are getting off the next station, you four will choose new seats that does not sit next to any of you all!"

Madeline was first to get up. "Fine, I don't want to be around the peanut gallery anyways," she bit back as she moved. Teff shook his head as he stared between the two women again.

"Me-ow," the man commented as Madeline walked away. Joshua rolled his eyes at the comment and got up as the rest did. Teff glanced between the three of them before he walked away. The woman stomped away first. As Joshua walked past the man, he tapped Joshua by his right pocket. Joshua turned, and the man gave a half smile as he stuffed his own hands in his pockets for a mere moment. "Hey, she's a real piece of work." The man took his hands out of his pockets and tapped hard against Joshua's right leg. "No hard feelings, right? No reason to leave the train with another pissed-off person on my list."

Joshua shrugged as he slid his hands in his own pockets. The ticket rubbed against his hand, which calmed him down. *At least I'm getting out of here,* he thought. "Yeah, no hard feelings."

The man slipped his own hands in his pocket and nodded with a charming smirk. "Good." He moved past Joshua and toward the back of the cart. Joshua followed him. Madeline grabbed him when he made it halfway down the aisle. She pulled him into the chairs in front of her as he heard the door open in the back of the cart. A man sat there next to him and stared at him curiously. Joshua gave an awkward smile and muttered an apology. The man said nothing, only stared at Joshua. Joshua's comfort depleted. The man had shaggy black hair and bright-blue eyes. His skin gleamed against the yellow light, almost as if it tanned him with the glow alone.

"What are you doing? We aren't allowed to sit near each other," Joshua hissed lowly toward Madeline.

"No, he said *next* to each other. Learn the difference," she snarked as she got comfortable in her seat. "Besides, I get off next anyways."

Joshua's eyes widened. "What? Next stop?" She nodded as a smile quivered on her lips.

"Y-yeah," she stuttered. "I-I don't think Teff would really be that hard on us. I'm a dead girl anyways. I'd like to at least talk to my friend."

Joshua grimaced at the comment yet nodded in reply. A loud clap took their attention to the back of the cart where Teff stood at the opened door. "All right, everyone! I am looking for glowing tickets! We are at station HL 5A! 5A! Station HL 5A!" Joshua's eyes glanced around the cart curiously. Two people got up from their seats. One man had a hard time as he tried to stand. The weight from his body seemed to pain him as it weighed him down. Joshua bit his lip uncomfortably as the man heaved himself into the aisle from the back of the cart. He waddled over to Teff and handed him the glowing ticket excitedly before he practically jumped off. Joshua and Madeline stared at the man as he exited in shock.

"Did he just…" Madeline's question trailed off as the man heaved off the cart.

"He was excited to leave," Joshua added in.

"That's what happens when you're as addicted to food as he is." The two jumped as they looked back at the man they sat next to. His calm smile never left his face as he gleamed back at the two.

"W-what do you mean?" Joshua asked as he took in a deep breath. His heart raced a million miles a minute from the shock. Something about the man did not rub Joshua right. There was an ominous vibe that came from the man's calm demeanor. *How can someone be so calm?* Joshua asked himself as he looked around the cart. "How do you know he was addicted to food?"

"He wouldn't stop asking Teff for some snacks," the man calmly explained. "I think he suffered from a binging disorder. Or a leptin fault. He did say that he could never feel full." The man's eyes glanced up to the ceiling in thought. "Then again, I guess you could also take that in a psychological sense too. Always trying to fill the void with something materialistic." He shrugged after a moment before his eyes stared back at the two. "Guess we'll never know." Joshua slowly nodded as his eyes darted back toward Teff. The conductor had his attention on very thin man that held the ticket with a deathlike grip. Joshua gulped as he turned back to the man that stared intently at him.

"Uh, yeah, that's an interesting way to think about it," Joshua rambled out.

"So who are you two? I'm Pedro," the man introduced.

"Joshua," he muttered.

"Madeline," she said, a bit more eager for a conversation.

"It's nice to meet you both," Pedro said as his smile grew by a fraction. Pedro turned his head back toward the window. "So what do you two think makes this place so…torturous?" Skepticism laced Pedro's voice. Joshua saw him as he judged the layout that surrounded them.

Madeline scooted over in her seat and got a better look. "Maybe you can't actually eat the food?" she asked in response.

"Maybe. That would be a way to torment someone," he agreed. "What do you think, Joshua?"

The question crawled down his back by the calm tone. He noticed the blue eyes that stared back at him through the reflection. They were calm and calculated as they stared at Joshua. He shrugged as he turned his attention away. "C-couldn't tell ya," he stuttered. His eyes focused on Teff as the conductor shut the door with a loud click. The man hummed as he went toward the front of the cart.

"Awe! Look how cute!" Madeline's awe fell onto Joshua's ears. He whipped his head and inched closer to the window. Between Pedro's and Madeline's heads, he saw something small and red moved. Arms and legs sprouted out of a sugar-covered gumdrop. A singular eye opened up as the heavy-set man from their cart took a cupcake flower. "They have little arms and legs!" Madeline exclaimed. Joshua leaned in a bit closer to the window. He saw the sweet, childlike smile that came from the gumdrop character that waddled up to the man. A smile formed on his face. The bell rang in his ears, but his eyes would not tear away from the cute creature.

"Yeah, he looks like something Sophie would buy for her stuffed plushy collection," he commented with a slight chuckle.

"Off we go!" Teff called aloud. They continued to watch the creature. It waddled up to the man, and the man gave it no mind as he munched on the cupcake. It stared at him for a few moments before a sinister smile grew on its face. The train roared to life as the gumdrop creature lunged toward the man. Sharp teeth clutched onto the man's neck. Blood gushed from the man's neck as he screamed in agony. Madeline covered her mouth as Joshua audibly gasped. The gumdrop tore off pieces of flesh and spat it aside as it continued. It started to go further down its neck as the train started to move. Other gumdrops popped up from different parts of the area and raced up to the screaming human. Joshua looked away as bile rushed up to his throat. He grabbed his throat as stomach acid burned against it. His head swam as his body swayed in wooziness.

"Oh my god," Madeline gasped out as she turned her head away. Pedro said nothing as he continued to watch out the window.

"That makes soooo much more sense," Joshua gagged out a few breaths.

"I really do hope that whatever hell I am going to does *not* do that," Madeline squirmed.

Thoughts of the succubus trailed in Joshua's mind. *All I can hope is that she treats you better when she gets you,* Joshua thought as he winced the thoughts of torn flesh away. He leaned his head against the back of the seat as the idea of vomiting slowly settled in his stomach. He took in deep breaths, and the vanilla scent calmed him. After a moment, his eyes opened. The yellow lights of the train ceiling glared back down at him. His head lolled to the side and noticed Madeline kept her head low while Pedro continued to stare out the window.

Chapter 12

Seeking Turned to Obsession...

THE TRAIN ROLLED ALONG the sugarcoated landscape for a while. An eerie silence fell over the cart as everyone sat with their own thoughts. Joshua's eyes glanced to Madeline from time to time. Her eyes remained on the floor as her head hung low. Joshua felt the need to say something to her, but he could not muster the words that sounded right. *What do I say to someone that is about to hit their final stop?* He pondered this question with a heavy heart. Madeline never struck him as a bad person by nature. Then again, from what he had understood from Teff, these tickets were based off what one was judged as. Not knowing her real life, he wondered if that was why he saw her as a nice person. "Odd," escaped his lips a bit too loudly.

"What's odd?" Madeline's voice cracked as she spoke.

His eyes fell on her again as he shook his head. "Nothing. Don't worry 'bout it. How are you feeling?"

She shrugged at the question. "As good as I can, I guess?" A chuckle of disbelief escaped her lips. "I just...I was always warned about what would happen if I kept doing what I did, but I never thought it would actually happen to me." She chuckled a bit more. "Isn't it weird? I don't think anyone thought any different from me on here. That they thought they could change starting tomorrow or that it wouldn't happen to them."

The words hit Joshua's heart. It pained him to watch the tears that trickled down her face. Drops of sadness fell from her cheeks and onto her lap. "Madeline," Joshua spoke up.

"I don't want to deal with this alone," she sobbed quietly. Her shoulders shook as tears streamed down her face. Her fiery hair covered most of her face away from him as her head drooped. "I don't want to go alone."

"Is everything all right over here?" Joshua jumped as Teff spoke from directly behind him. His hand gripped his shirt over his chest and turned around. Teff chuckled amusedly at Joshua's reaction. His eyes fluttered up to Madeline, and the smile slowly left his face. An understanding frown tugged at Teff's lips as he sat into the seat next to Madeline. Joshua witnessed the event unfold before him. Madeline furiously wiped her tears away as her attention turned toward Teff.

"Hey now," Teff said gently as he brought a hand up to her face. He wiped away a tear that formed in her eye. "Pretty girls like you shouldn't cry." Teff's hand fell to his lap as Madeline chuckled bitterly.

"Pretty?" she asked, disgusted. "About as pretty as a rat." She wiped another tear away that formed in her eye. "You know, I used to be called either super pretty or an ugly witch on social media all the time. How can anyone see this mess as pretty? I was fat most of my life and always had an ugly look to me." She laughed ruefully. "And in the end, I'm alone down here. Going straight to hell like everyone told me I would." Her hand messily pushed red hair from her face, and Joshua saw the puffy eyes and grim expression clearly.

"Would my opinion make any difference?" Teff asked.

Madeline shrugged. "I don't know anymore." She took a deep breath as Teff hooked one leg over the other and placed his hands neatly on his lap.

"Well, I personally believe that you are beautiful," Teff started. "And I don't mean just for your looks either. You obsessed too much with your looks in the living world, but did you ever notice that the people that held you closest probably never once cared at all?" Madeline stiffened as her ears listened and mind thought through his words. "Even now, even in the afterlife, you have at least one friend to help you on the journey." Teff nodded over to Joshua and smiled kindly to Madeline. "And you may be spitfire, but I found that you were not an ugly witch or a waste of time. Instead, you are just another lost soul that got dealt a hard hand. The harsh truth is some are dealt great hands in life and some are dealt horrible ones. Sometimes the deck needs reshuffling, sometimes we bet too much, and sometimes we don't double down when we know we should. No soul is ever dealt the same hand twice, and that is the only thing assured to us."

Madeline giggled after a moment. "Poker references. Heh, my dad used to use those references all the time."

Teff nodded as his warm smile grew wider. "And I have a feeling he would have agreed with me," Teff added.

"Maybe."

Teff used his fingers to brush some hair out of his own eyes as he leaned back in his seat. "And if you are afraid to take the first step into the afterlife, I can get off with you and make sure you are where you need to be."

Madeline perked up at Teff's offer. "B-but why? I was such a… well, a witch."

"I have met many souls in my lifetime. I understand that everyone processes death differently. If I got offended by you, I would really be terrible at this job." Madeline giggled at the comment. "If I remember correctly, your stop is next?" Teff asked. Her giggle died down in her throat as she nodded. "Then I will make sure that you are comforted on your way out."

"Thank you, Teff."

He nodded as his eyes glanced to the window. Joshua followed the gaze. The skies darkened as they fell into a nightscape. "I will be back," Teff said lowly as he stood with a loud groan. "God, I know better than to sit down!" His arms raised over his head as he stretched. "I get way too comfortable!" After another stretch, he continued his route up the aisle.

Joshua turned his attention back to Madeline and saw that the sadness melted from her, and a content smile grew in its place. "Feeling better?" Joshua asked.

"Actually, yeah," Madeline said after a moment of thought. "I feel at peace somehow."

"That makes sense," Pedro spoke up. Joshua perked his attention over to the man's calm demeanor.

"What do you mean makes sense?" Joshua asked.

"Don't you know?" Pedro asked. "It is always said that the Grim Reaper always causes souls to feel at peace." Pedro pointed over to the train conductor with a crooked finger. "That is basically our Grim Reaper." Madeline hummed as they both thought it over.

"Well, yeah," Madeline admitted, "but since I'm already here, I don't think I mind Teff as my Grim Reaper. He is not nearly as gothic or scary as stories made people like him to believe." Joshua agreed. Pedro shrugged and sat back in his seat. "Aren't you scared of where you're going?"

"Yeah, you seem really calm," Joshua added.

The man shook his head. "I knew where I was going long before I got here. I've made my decisions on the surface, and I don't regret them. So my sentence is mine, and I own up to it. I cannot stand people that would try to steal or switch tickets on here. I heard some whispers of it earlier, but I just don't see the point. Your sentence is meant for you and you alone. Why change it? You earned it."

Joshua hummed as he thought it over. After a long pause, he agreed. "Yeah, I guess you do have to earn it no matter where you go."

Pedro pointed to Joshua. "Exactly."

"So where are you going?" Madeline asked.

"Let's just keep it at...further down than you," Pedro stated with a small smile, a smile that sent chills straight through Joshua's body.

Madeline nodded and chose not to push it any further as she averted her eyes to the window. Joshua saw her puzzled face in the reflection. "Stars?" she asked, stunned.

Joshua and Pedro's attention peered toward the window. Their gazes looked upward. Little specks of light sparkled through the pitch-black sky. The three awed over the beauty of them. Small balls of light that glimmered through the sky was an anomaly in Joshua's eyes. The train slowed down into a slow stroll as they continued to stare at the lights. The train stopped. Joshua continued to stare out at the star-covered night sky. His eyes could not tear away no matter how hard he tried. The only thing that steered him from the sight was the tap on his shoulder. Annoyance fluttered inside his chest as he turned. Teff gave him a sympathetic smile before he pointed at Madeline with his pointer finger. "Would you also like to walk your friend off the train?"

Joshua scrunched his brows together. "You didn't give me that option with Tiffany," he replied sharply.

"You tried to take her place. Not only that, she also did not want an escort either."

Joshua lowered his gaze for a moment, and then it fell on Madeline. Her eyes sparkled as she looked up to the sky. A smile cracked across his face. His head answered for him with a nod as he stood. Teff gazed at him for a moment.

"Oh," Teff added, "don't think you're special. I've offered a few people to escort the friends that they made here out. You're only special because you are the only one that said yes."

"I never saw you talk to others at the stop outside of calling for a ticket," Joshua argued.

"I talked to them in transit. You guys weren't the only souls I got to interact with on this train." Joshua stood and glanced down at the entranced Madeline. "I think she would rather appreciate the gesture though. Leave a soul at peace."

He used three fingers and lightly poked her on her shoulder. Her eyelids fluttered as she shook her head. She glanced at Joshua and then at Teff. The color fell from her face for a moment before she cleared her throat. Her hand dug for the ticket that laid in her pocket. She held it with a deathlike grip as she pulled it out. It glowed the same ethereal white color. Madeline glared at the ticket for a moment before she took a final breath and handed it to Teff's extended hand. He took it gently from her and waited for her to stand. "Aren't you going to announce to the rest of the train?" Madeline asked. Trepidation laid in her tone as she slowly stood alongside Joshua.

They looked around the train and noticed a common trend. Everyone stared starstruck out the windows and up the sky.

"I think the demons in the sky will have them entertained for long enough," Teff admitted with a huff. His eyes scanned the train before it went back to Madeline. "Besides, I had to keep track of the tickets. Between here and the next station, there is only one getting off at both." Teff's eyes fell back on Madeline. "We're ready when you are."

Madeline's eyes widened as they targeted Joshua. "*You* are coming too?" she asked him, stunned.

"Teff gave me the option," he admitted as he scratched the back of his head. "And besides, you and I would have been great friends. I think we are even pretty good friends now." A bit of anxiety weighed down his body as Madeline stared at him in shock. *Oh god, does she not want me to?* Anxiety filled his thoughts as her eyes fell to the floor. After a long moment, a smile of relief brightened her face as she looked back at the two.

"Thanks, guys," she said softly. She took in a deep breath and walked into the aisle. Joshua followed behind her and Teff behind him. They slowly made their way to the back of the train. Joshua's feet felt cemented to the ground as he forced himself forward. When they got to the back door, the scene before them did not seem harmful.

Long grass drifted against the wind. A dark landscape laid before them that was lit by the star-like creatures above. There were no screams of terror, no movement outside of the whistling wind, nothing but silence. Joshua gulped. A feeling crept up his spine that something had to be watching them from out there. This was hell. In his eyes, something had to be wrong. He clenched his jaw in worry as Madeline glanced back at them.

Teff's chuckle rang in Joshua's ears. "HL 5B. We are at HL 5B," he said quietly with mirth.

"Why are you saying that now?" Madeline asked as her voice shook.

"I feel that there is a certain charm to it to let the souls know what substation they are at. To know that there is really worse than yours out there somewhere. For some, it's comforting," Teff explained. A morbid calm fell over Joshua and Madeline.

Creepy as hell, but…it is comforting to know that her stop isn't the worst, Joshua thought.

Madeline looked at Joshua, and he stared back at her. She bit her cheek as she turned around. "Ready, Joshua?" she asked fearfully.

"Whenever you are," he said. His voice gave away his fear and caution, yet Madeline ignored it. She took in a deep breath and took her first step off the train. He followed behind her and heard Teff's footsteps behind him. The air was cool on his skin as he walked out. Everything around them was dyed in a silvery color against the natural environment. Madeline's head swiveled as she took further steps out. A hand stopped Joshua from following her. He turned around and saw Teff as he shook his head. Joshua cocked his brow, and Teff motioned his head toward Madeline. Joshua turned around and noticed that Madeline stood in the middle of the clearing. Her eyes gazed at the creatures in the sky. "I don't understand," Joshua said quietly to himself.

"The demons here are not merciful, I assure you," Teff replied just as quietly.

Soft footsteps perked his ears. He gasped as he glanced to the right and saw a creature that made him internally scream. It looked like a human, but its skin clung to its body. Every bone poked out against its skin. Its eyes were dark voids with small balls of lights in the sockets. Its arms swung at its side like it was detached from its body. Its jaw was slacked and hung as if unhinged. It made its way slowly to her. Joshua opened his mouth and waved a hand toward Madeline. A hand clamped over his mouth and pulled his head back. His head collided with the train with a loud thud. Teff kept his hand over Joshua's mouth as he brought a finger up to his lips. A shush whistled from his lips. Joshua stared between the creature and Madeline. When it got in arm's length of Madeline, Teff took his hand away and motioned for Joshua to get back on the train.

"But Made—"

"She will be fine," Teff whispered as he interjected. He used his hand and forced Joshua back on the train.

Joshua fell to the ground, shocked at Teff's strength. Joshua got on to his elbows as Teff climbed aboard. The thing got closer to Madeline. When it reached out to touch her, the door slammed shut with a loud click. He glared at Teff. "What the hell is that thing?" Joshua asked, outraged. "That thing looks like a damn zombie!" Anger overthrew his anxiety as he stood on his feet. Teff motioned for Joshua to get back to his seat with a simple flick of his wrist.

"Will you please be more civil?" Teff asked, annoyed.

"But you aren't answering me!"

"I intend to if you stop it with the anger nonsense." Teff kept an indifferent glare toward Joshua as the boy breathed.

Joshua made his way back down the cart and to his seat next to Pedro. As he glanced around the cart, everyone's eyes were still on the sky that was blanketed with starry creatures. Teff strolled past Joshua and up toward the bell. His attention glanced down to his pocket watch before he shook his head and rang the bell. No one moved or made any attempt to. Joshua stared wildly around the train. "What is wrong with everyone?" Joshua asked his thought aloud. The train jumped forward with life. No one seemed to notice except for him.

"The demons are those stars in the sky," Teff said as his own eyes glanced around at everyone. "They are a horrible thing, really." He slowly crept back up the aisle and made effort to not stare out any windows. "They enrapture people with their glowing light, like a moth to a flame." Teff concentrated his stare on Joshua as he slowly made his way closer. "And just like a moth to a flame, get too close and you get burned. However, in this case, getting burned is starving your soul of energy and being turned into nothing better than mindless zombies. Former shadows of oneself." Teff leaned on the seat in front of Joshua. "That thing you saw out there was a starved soul."

"Souls starve?" Joshua asked.

"Just like the rest of the world, the soul needs energy to function. It's why most still kept their shape of their former mortal bodies while they are down here. Starving a soul just to keep their attention is a hell made to a very select few. However, more souls are being sent to this substation." Teff flicked his wrist dismissively. "Something called social media is an absolute catalyst for this realm. In fact, it's almost fascinating how some are so starved for attention. So much so that their punishment—"

"Is to literally starve themselves because they aren't paying attention," Joshua finished Teff's statement. His jaw fell as realization dawned on him. "Her social media." His eyes glared at Teff. "She wasn't doing anything wrong! She thought she was helping people!"

"And I didn't call her judgment. Neither did you."

Joshua felt a pang in his heart as Teff said the words. "How could anyone ever—"

"You are too naive, Joshua," Teff interjected. Teff pushed away from the seat that he leaned against. "You assume that because you have met them here that the way they acted here was how they acted in real life. I can assure you, the judgment is rather fair, and everyone deserves where they go." Teff continued his walk back to the front of the cart. "And who knows? Maybe that succubus will whisk her away like she wanted to earlier. She may get a lighter sentence out of pure coincidence." Teff shrugged. "It depends on her hand."

He did not look back. When he got to the front of the cart, he took his seat where Madeline sat before and leaned against it. Joshua sat back on his seat with a soft bump against the chair. His eyes glanced out toward the moving scenery. A flash of blond caught his eyes against the silvery scene. Joshua pushed up in his chair and caught a better view of a person before they got too far away. His eyes caught her. The blond hair and leather outfit was unmistakable to him. A relieved smile cracked on his face. "Hopefully, a lighter sentence," Joshua mumbled to himself as he sat relaxed back in his seat. He felt his pocket and felt the paper from outside the material. A small sigh escaped him. "I hope for it anyways."

Chapter 13

But It's Quality!

THE SKY BLED INTO a powdery blue as the train rushed along. Once the stars faded into sandy-colored clouds, people shook their heads. Dazed eyes glanced around the room as they mumbled and whispered lowly. Joshua looked around. Besides Pedro and him, few other people remained. They all sat in separate seats on the cart. No one sat close to the front where Teff remained. In fact, besides Pedro and him, no one even sat next to each other. His attention turned to Pedro as he shook himself out of his daze. Joshua cleared his throat as an awkwardness weighed down on his head.

"You doing okay?" Joshua asked awkwardly. *God, he must think I'm still weird for sitting here,* he thought.

"Yeah, it was like I got cotton in my brain!" Pedro exclaimed. "How about you?" Joshua shrugged. Pedro turned his head back toward the empty seats behind him. A frown cracked on his face as he noticed the seats remained empty. "Where did she go?"

"The last stop was hers," Joshua explained grimly. He winced as the thought of the starving soul came to mind.

"And she didn't even say goodbye. Hm, rude." Pedro shrugged as he sighed and relaxed back in his seat. "Oh, well. Life moves on." His head cocked as the statement left his lips. "Well, afterlife."

Joshua cleared his throat as he glanced around the train again. The thought of switching seats became appealing to him as he witnessed how far apart people sat. He cleared his throat again and rubbed the back of his neck. "Hey, would you want me to move? I didn't know if it actually bothered you that I sat here next to you," Joshua said awkwardly.

Pedro waved him off. "Nah, you're fine. I didn't even notice. Besides, I like the company. Right before you got dragged down, someone else that sat there got off the station before." Joshua slowly nodded. "So tell me about yourself. I always loved learning about people." The calm demeanor caused Joshua to shudder a bit.

"W-well what would you wanna know?"

"You seem young for this train ride," Pedro commented as his eyes trailed over Joshua casually. "What got you here?"

"I…I really don't remember," Joshua admitted. "Every time I try to remember, my head kills me."

Pedro's eyebrow cocked up, intrigued. "Well, what was life like in the living world? Were you sick? Cancer?"

"Why do you wanna know?"

"I've always been fascinated by people. The way their emotions made them impulsive and dependent on their environment always fascinated me. I loved it especially when they were in fear. You learn so much about people when they are afraid."

Joshua's back stiffened as a cold spell washed over him. The joy from Pedro's voice made Joshua cringe. "Tell you what, I'll tell you why I'm here if you tell me about yourself. Call it a trade for a trade." Joshua slowly took in a breath. Curiosity swam through his head as he looked closer at the man. In fact, a part of him almost looked familiar. Pedro smiled calmly as Joshua stared at him. *I've seen you before,* Joshua thought. *But where?*

"Well, I was your average band kid," he started. His shoulders hunched into him as he slouched in his seat. "I got the crap kicked outta me a lot, but I typically went through school without being noticed." Joshua shrugged as he sighed. "Can't say life was peachy, but it sure a hell of a lot better than it being gone. At least, I'm realizing that the more I'm on here." His eyes rolled around the cart. "Now thinking about it, I remember feeling…sad. All the time."

"Why?" Pedro asked. His attention homed in on Joshua as he leaned forward. Joshua glanced at him to realize that Pedro seemed more fascinated than anything with the emotion.

"W-well," Joshua continued hesitantly, "like I said, I got bullied a lot. That and my family could never afford anything. I remember that we were so poor one year that I searched for money on the streets or in the change slots of vending machines so I could buy Sophie, my little sis, a teddy bear. It was the only present she got that year, but I think my parents were grateful."

"Tell me more," Pedro stated, enraptured by the conversation. His smile widened.

"Yeah, I wasn't a happy kid. In fact, I think I was depressed, but I never told anyone. No one...no one wanted to listen. I was certain of that." A frown fell on Joshua's face. A familiar sadness slowed his heart. A tightness gripped his chest, but it was not anxiety. The weight of a ton of bricks lined his shoulders as sadder memories flooded back through his mind. "I used to hang out at this bridge when I got sad." The thought of calm water flowed through his head, but it did not bring him peace. Instead, dread flooded his mind. "I would go there when I couldn't go home. You know, there are just times where you just can't go home because it was too much?" Joshua glanced over and saw Pedro's stare almost turned hungry as he listened. Pedro nodded. Joshua gulped but continued. "Well... that was my life sometimes. And it's weird...'cause the place used to bring me peace." A thought came to his mind, a small whisper that he could not hear.

"And why not now?"

Emotions brought an intense pressure behind Joshua's eyes as the dull ache resurfaced in his head. He searched his memories, but not one moment came to mind where the answer was a clear choice. The pressure piled up in his head. It was about to burst. "It had to be done" was all that repeated through his head. "I...don't know," Joshua choked out. He gasped as tears unconsciously streamed from his eyes.

"Well, obviously a part of you does," Pedro stated hungrily.

"If it does, it isn't saying anything," Joshua bit back. Pedro's eyes widened in surprise. "Sorry," he mumbled.

"You know, memories are suppressed more when they are traumatic," Pedro said as he took a deep breath. He turned back in his seat and relaxed. The hunger slowly subsided in his eyes when he looked back at Joshua. "That was probably where you died. Your soul remembers the emotion, but your mind does not want to cooperate yet."

Joshua slowly nodded. "I'll have to think that over a bit," Joshua muttered.

"Please do. When you find out, let me know," Pedro chimed happily.

Joshua glared at him for a moment. "Duly noted." Joshua turned his attention more toward the calm man after another long breath. "So what about you?" Pedro quirked a brow. "A trade for a trade. I wanna learn about you now."

Pedro hummed and nodded his head. "Well, I guess you could say I was a—"

"All right, everyone! We are stopping at HL 5C! Get your ticket ready! We are stopping at HL 5C!" Teff stated with glee. Pedro brought up a finger as his head swiveled toward the window.

"Let me get back to you on that. I love to witness all the floors," Pedro explained.

Joshua viewed out the window in the seats ahead of them. Sand covered the ground around them. A bright reddish-orange sun beat down on the landscape. Joshua craned his head more toward the window and saw a gigantic box in the horizon. It glowed a bright white that was as blinding as the sun. Joshua blinked rapidly as he stared at it. When dots cluttered the edges of his eyes, his head swayed away from the window. He rubbed his eyes with his sleeves as a groan escaped his throat. "Damn, that's blinding," he muttered as his eyes blinked away the spots.

"Well, we're about to go in it!" Pedro exclaimed as his body shifted closer to the window. "Seems to be an entryway in."

"Why the hell would you put a random box in the middle of a desert?" Joshua asked aloud.

"I mean, it is hell, Josh," Pedro stated after a moment. Joshua's eyes concentrated on the back of the seat ahead of him as he thought about it. "Kinda the job here to create nightmares that make no sense."

Joshua's shoulders lifted into a half shrug. His attention turned toward the shuffling around the front of the train. Teff held his arms over his head and stretched as he stood. The train conductor's silver eyes scanned the cart. Joshua noticed the sigh that escaped his lips as he trailed slowly toward the back of the cart. Teff's eyes focused on no one in particular as he watched the people that were left. *One is supposed to be getting off here,* Joshua thought as he turned around and slowly observed the cart. *Who is it though? No one even seems nervous.* Before Joshua could survey the cart, the train jumped. Joshua hopped forward in his seat, and his head whipped toward the window. A wall of white greeted his eyes as they sped by. The train roared as it sped through. Joshua took in a deep breath as he shifted back into his seat. Pedro stayed glued to the window. Joshua looked away as he felt the train slow down. It pushed his torso forward lightly. He dug his fingers into his seat as he leaned further forward.

"All right, everyone! HL 5C! We are at HL 5C! For the lucky patron, have your ticket ready!" Teff exclaimed as he passed Joshua. The train stopped.

"What?" Pedro asked under his breath. Joshua heard the hiss from Pedro, and his body turned toward the man. Pedro leaned back in his seat as a piece of dark hair fell in his face. "That sucks."

Joshua cocked his head. "What is it?"

"I understand what this is. It isn't anything that will interest us." Joshua cocked his brow. Pedro's head nodded toward the window. "Switch with me and take a look. You'll see what I mean."

His curiosity alluded him as he agreed to switch seats. Joshua awkwardly shifted over Pedro. Pedro slid underneath Joshua and into the other seat. Joshua's gaze turned toward the window. What he saw outside alluded him as he slowly sat down. The area was entirely white. The floors, ceiling, and walls were all a bland white, nothing like the first station that they went to in heaven. This was dull and lifeless. Nothing glittered or gleamed. However, there was an odd thing that caused Joshua's hairs to stand on end. People floated in above the ground cross-legged. They wore white robes with a dark-red eye imprinted on the chests. They were all bald, eyes closed, and red beads sat around their necks. Joshua shook in his seat as he stared at one in particular. It bobbed up and down as it levitated off the ground. White eyelids opened, and dark-red eyes reflected back at him. The eyes showed no malice or anything frightful. In fact, they were calm and peaceful. It bobbed against the ground a few more times before it stood on the ground. Eyes opened up from the rows of people around it. Red eyes peered at the train calmly. Everyone stood exactly at the same time.

"What the hell is this?" a woman shouted somewhere behind Joshua. His eyes tore away from window and behind him. Clarice, the woman that sat behind Madeline and him earlier, swore as Teff raised his hands calmly.

"I said, your ticket is glowing, and that this is your stop," Teff explained in a low tone, a thing that Joshua noticed was very uncharacteristic to the train conductor's usual flamboyant style.

"You said you would talk to management about my ticket!" Clarice argued.

Teff shook his head with a heavy sigh. "And I never heard anything back."

The sound of a low hum rumbled through Joshua's ears. His head whipped back and saw the group of people shut their eyes, all except the one that opened his eyes first. They all hummed. Joshua felt an uneasiness settled in his throat as he watched them. His eyes widened. A third eye opened in the center of all their heads that resembled a burnt orange. Six eyes also opened around the center of the forehead eye. The six eyes' pupils were dilated unlike the forehead eye in the center. Joshua grunted in disgust as the man with his eyes opened walked toward the train slowly. His forehead eye looked along the train as he walked up to the cart. The man cut out of Joshua's view, but he heard the knock on the exit door. A gulp choked in Joshua's throat as his head slowly looked back. The knock was soft and subtle yet somehow louder than the woman that complained. Everyone turned their attention to the back of the cart like clockwork. Joshua took in a deep breath as he tried to steady his quickened heartbeat. Teff walked over to the back of the cart and opened the door with a calm, soft smile.

"Nokoiyma," Teff said quietly, yet it rang clear in Joshua's ears.

"Nokoiyma," his own mouth, along with everyone else on the train, repeated. His body did not feel like his own as his head tilted respectively toward the eight-eyed man that stepped further onto the train.

"Kikya," a deep voice stated. A tension fell upon Joshua's shoulders as his head raised like a puppet with strings. All eight eyes moved around the cart in different directions. "Relax, my children. I am not here for most of you today," the person said with calm assurance. This oddly caused the heavy feeling in him to subside. His anxiety was forced in a corner away from his mind. Joshua's eyes glanced to Teff and saw that he lingered around the exit way with his eyes focused on anything outside of the man that entered. "You were told to exit the train," the calm, deep voice stated.

Joshua's eyes turned toward the man as he strolled up to Clarice. Clarice stood defiant as her chest puffed out. "I want to speak to management!" she stated it proudly, like her life was not over and could have a redo. Joshua sat there amazed at how entitled she seemed to be. "My ticket was screwed up. I was supposed to go to heaven!" She crossed her arms over her chest and stared the man down. All eight eyes focused on her as a frown fell on his face.

"Defiance does not suit you, my child."

"I am *not* your child!" The woman bit back. "I want an explanation as to why I should even bother getting off with you."

Joshua bit his lower lip as he saw the person clenched their jaw. The person glanced back at Teff, and Teff looked away. *What the hell is this?* Joshua asked himself silently. A dilated eye shifted toward him before it turned back toward the woman. A gasp was stifled in Joshua's throat.

"My child, I—"

"I said I am not your child."

"But you *are* a child," the person sneered back. The patient exterior fell away from the man. An angry tension filled the air that made it hard to breathe. "And you, child, are sent here to join my regime. To rehabilitate. To become new. To become one of the rest." The person motioned toward the group that laid outside of the train. A charming smile fell on the person's face that chilled Joshua to the bone. "You can become something more than yourself. Would that not be perfect? To be part of something more? To be connected through me?" The eye in the center of his head dilated. The man licked its teeth, which were no different from razor blades. There was a hunger in its eyes as it gazed over the woman. Joshua stared between the woman and the creature that barely looked human. She swayed as she stood. Her posture slacked as her eyelids dazed down. Her eyes concentrated on the eye in the center of its forehead. Her hands laid limp at her side as her feet glided a bit closer to the person.

The hungry smile turned wider. It became inhumane and deranged as the person cocked its head sideways. It brought up a hand and held her head. "Finally, you can stop fighting," the deep voice said without the lips ever moving. It moved its thumb to the center of the head and pressed in. The woman did not move or show pain as the sounds of bone cracking turned Joshua rigid. Bone splintered through the skin. Blood splattered out as bone chipped out like fragmentation. Joshua shuddered at the sight of blood. Joshua stared at the woman. She never flinched. In fact, she took the infliction like he did nothing more than tap her on the forehead. As he let go of her, blood drooled down from her face. Her eyes were bloodshot, but her face was relaxed. Blood dripped down from her face, and droplets stained her dark-gray clothes and the carpet underneath her. Joshua noticed the ticket that glowed as it laid on the ground. A few droplets of blood splashed against the ticket, yet nothing stained it. The blood beaded up and slid off the ticket. It fascinated Joshua.

Must be some fancy paper, Joshua thought.

"Let us go, my child." The words whipped Joshua's attention back to the two. It held out a hand toward the woman. The woman numbly nodded as she grabbed the hand with a deathlike grip. Her face dribbled more with blood as she smiled toward it. The person's smile turned kind, almost human, as it turned around and led her off the cart. No one moved or spoke as they left.

Teff refused to lift his own eyes until the cart door was softly shut with the distinct click that locked it. Once they were off, Joshua let out a breath that he did not realize he held. Teff walked ahead and grabbed the ticket that laid on the ground and inspected the glow. His eyebrow raised as he read over the back of the ticket before he shrugged and shoved it in his pocket. Joshua turned his attention to the window as Teff moved toward the front of the cart. He found the woman as she was surrounded by eight-eyed people. They held thumbs to different parts of her face and indented into her skull, which left fresh, bloody holes in their wake. Joshua grimaced as his stomach dropped. Blood fell from the woman's face. She cackled in response to the blood as she touched her own face and looked toward the ground. Blood steadily pooled around her feet as it streamed off her face. Her cackle turned into howling laughter. Joshua pushed his hands into his ears to block out the noise. His head spun as anxiety overcame him again.

The laughter echoed in his head as he pressed tighter against his ears and squeezed his eyes shut. He barely heard the bell as it rang against the laughter or the train that breathed life as it lunged forward. He barely noticed the hand that touched his shoulder as he tried to shut the laughter out. His head echoed it so loud that it drowned out his heartbeat as it raced through his chest and up his throat. He pushed his head into the back of the seat in front of him and clawed at his ears. "Stop it…" Joshua croaked out lowly. The laughter turned from the woman to something more familiar: the laughter of other kids. "Stop it." The laughter grew louder as he squeezed his eyes shut tighter. Pain pressed against his head and throbbed. The laughter turned from a sound to a vision of kids from school as they laughed at him. They crowded around him. "Stop. It," he growled as he felt the cold water that soaked his clothes and the feathers that covered his face. "*Stop it!*"

"*Josh!*" A light blow to the head rammed Joshua into the window. He groaned as he furiously glared toward Pedro. A demented grin grew on Pedro's face as he stared at Joshua. Fascination filled his features as he glowed. He stared at Joshua like Joshua was a fantastic science experiment, a specimen to be watched and admired. After a moment, Pedro cleared his throat and took in a few deep breaths. "Sorry, sorry. Couldn't help myself. I just…I wanted to be a part of the emotional outrage."

"Emotional outrage?"

"Yeah! You were freaking out, kid," Pedro breathed in deeply. Joshua slowly nodded. "Guessing this substation really brought back memories?" After a moment, Joshua nodded.

"Y-yeah, sort of," Joshua mumbled.

"Anything worth sharing with the class?" Pedro asked, clearly enthused.

"Not yet. It didn't even make sense." Pedro frowned for a moment before he shrugged and nodded.

"Yeah, that makes sense. Oh well." Pedro sat back in his seat and looked out toward the rest of the cart. "Oh, by the way, your ticket is kinda peeping out of your pocket. I'd keep a better eye on it if I were you."

Joshua glanced down at his pocket and glared at the ticket. After a moment of thought, he brought it out. What he saw on the ticket drowned his emotions like he were captured under ice. Pedro glanced over his shoulder and gasped in shock. Joshua's hands shook as the ticket fell in his lap. His ticket was switched.

Chapter 14

Silence Is Deadly

JOSHUA SHOOK, BUT HE could not tell if it was fear or rage. It was a fight in his heart for dominance as he saw his ticket. END was written in big, bold letters. His memory danced around as he tried to figure out where he heard that from. Was it Jason? He shook his head. In his mind, that was the least of his concerns. A better question plagued his mind as he flipped the ticket every which way. Nothing was written on it except for END on the front. *How? I was so careful!* Joshua jabbed himself in the leg with his fist as anger ran rampant through him. *How?*

"Uh, Joshua? That's…I don't think you have the right ticket," Pedro admitted. His hand fished through the pocket of his dark-gray trousers and turned up with a ticket exactly like his. "Looks like someone duped you."

Joshua gritted his teeth. "How?" Joshua growled lowly to himself.

"Well, other than that one chic, did you ever rehand out your ticket?" Pedro asked.

No was the firm response given by Joshua. He combed his mind as his eyes searched the cart. There were only so few passengers left. Six of them remained. For a moment, Joshua could not fathom how many started out on this train cart, and now there were only six that stayed.

"Well, let's see. Did you move prior to sitting with me?" Pedro asked.

Joshua looked back at him, astonished. "Are you really going to try to help me figure it out?" was Joshua's rebuttal.

Pedro grinned. "Hey, I do have morals. Like I said before, I wouldn't try to take your ticket because I think the life you lived proved where the hell you were supposed to be. That's not just me personally. I think that way for everyone. I at least have that moral even in the afterlife. Course I'll help. Besides, how hard could it be? There are only six sorry saps on the train and only two more areas to go. Can't be *that* hard to narrow it down."

"Wait, how do you know there are only two more areas?" Joshua asked suspiciously.

Pedro chuckled as he pointed toward the window. "I've been sightseeing. You pick up the trend the more in depth you look at these levels. They follow a trend."

"That being?"

"The deadly sins," he said plainly. "You know, lust, sloth, all that crap. They were basically over personified representations if you really looked at it. Just categorized a bit differently." He shrugged. "Personally, I would have made it a bit more straightforward and just sent you to a pit, but hey, I didn't make the rules. I just go with them."

Joshua slowly nodded. Throughout this whole journey, nothing like that ever sprung to his mind. "So...where were we just now? Which one?"

"My guess?" Pedro asked. Joshua nodded. "Gluttony. Those gumdrop killers were a real showstopper." Pedro chuckled a bit in fondness as he reflected. "Coulda sworn they were my own kids by how they were eating them."

"You're a cannibal?" Joshua squeaked.

Pedro hummed before a light lit up in his eyes. "Oh, that's right! We never got to talk about me yet, huh?" Joshua slowly shook his head. "Yeah, I'm that...aw, what did they call me? It was all over the news at one point. The social killer? Something like that."

"You're the media maniac?"

"Yeah, that!" Pedro said with a snap. "Had a good ring to it honestly. Media did me justice there."

"I knew you looked familiar!" Joshua exclaimed. "You killed like ten different people! No one could even track you because of your coded IP addresses. How did you…why did you…*how* did you die?"

Pedro winced at the question. "Eh, the bitch I was fishing had a jealous husband. I was dead on arrival as soon as I met up with her down by her family's cabin. I wanna say she was supposed to ride with me, buuuuut"—Pedro motioned to the cart—"I have a feeling she just got hit again and lived. I remember the photos she would show me of the abuse. God, they were brutal. And I thought I was bad!"

"Why did you kill those people?"

"A snack really. I can't help it! When I get to know them and they get all emotional, I get so excited. I just want to live their emotions. I want to devour the fear that they accumulate when they realize what I'm going to do to them. The terror, the disgust, the anger, I love it. All of it." His mouth salivated as he spoke, and Joshua cringed inwardly. "I just wish I coulda had a bite of her," he admitted through gritted teeth. "That damn twelve gauge stopped me dead in my tracks." He snapped his fingers. "Oh well," he finished with a heavy sigh. His eyes glanced back down at Joshua's ticket and grunted. "But yeah, I'll help you with your ticket problems."

"Not gonna lie, never thought I would get help from a known serial killer," Joshua admitted.

"Hey, help comes from strange places sometimes. My first killing, someone actually helped me hide the body for me to get later *because* she hated the guy. Couldn't deny that hiding it on her farm was very helpful."

"Huh" was all Joshua could say.

"So you move much prior to sitting with me?"

"No, actually, I didn't really move much at all."

Pedro slowly nodded. He hummed as his eyes fell to the floor. Joshua glanced toward the window and saw the dimensional portal's bright blue glow against the dull white walls that encapsulated the train. "I know you sat next to the girl behind us because she dragged you over here, so it wasn't her. She got off," Pedro said thoughtfully.

"The other woman was the one that just got off with the…eye thingy," Joshua cringed.

"So who else was around you?" Pedro asked.

Joshua glanced around the cart and settled his eyes on the man that sat in the back of the train. The man sat there as cool as a cucumber as his eyes trailed to the window. Joshua paled. Memory came to mind of how they bumped into each other earlier when they switched seats. "Him," Joshua stated grimly as his head nodded toward the man at the window in the far back on the opposite side of the train. Pedro glanced back before he nodded slowly, and they both turned back around.

"This gives a whole new definition to it's always the quiet ones," Joshua muttered under his breath.

"Don't worry. We'll find a way to get it back," Pedro said quietly. His chair groaned as he leaned back and kicked his leg up over the other in silent contemplation.

The train pushed forward, and the outskirts of balls of light came into Joshua's view. Deep breaths escaped through his lungs as he joined Pedro in relaxing back in his seat. Memories started to swirl in his head as his eyes drifted shut. *What am I going to do?* he asked himself silently. *I need to find a way to get off this train. I have so much to change when I get off. Please, if any god is listening, please help.*

Chapter 15

Rage-Quit!

"LOOK! HE'S ALL COVERED in feathers!"

"Wow, he's a real idiot for falling for that one!"

"Hahaha! Wait till Haley gets a look at this!"

"Duuuuude, this is so going viral!" Everyone laughed as Joshua sat in a daze. Chlorine choked at his lungs and nose as he coughed up water. His head swam. His body felt heavy and wet. When his eyes glanced down, white tiles greeted his eyes along with a pool of water that dripped off him. A few soaked yellow feathers gripped to his arms and shirt. The scent of chlorine burned his nose. As he looked up, people swarmed around him. Some eyes laughed in glee, while others cast down their disdain. A cold shiver shook through his body as air conditioning blew down on him from above. He stood as others continued to point and mock at him.

I remember this, he said silently to himself. *They all laughed at me.*

Anxiety gripped his heart as fear plagued his mind. His feet carried him as he ran out of the pool area of the gym. The thoughts of being soaking wet on an autumn day did not pass Joshua's mind as he ran out of the school. His beaten-down car sat at the edge of the parking lot farthest from the school's gymnasium entrance. Feathers flew off him as he ran. "Fucking idiots!" Joshua growled as he ripped any excess yellow feathers off himself. "What did I ever do to deserve that?" His legs pumped as hard as they could so he could get to his car. His sanctuary. His curly hair was plastered to his head, and water got in his eyes. He angrily brushed away at his eyes as he got to his car. The cobalt blue of the beaten-down 2008 Pontiac G6 came into view. The laughter still filled his ears as he dragged himself inside the car and turned it on. The car hesitated but came to life slowly. Tears streamed down Joshua's face as the sounds of laughter still resonated inside his head. His hand gripped on the volume and blared whatever the rock station played to get his mind off it. "Stop it!" he screamed at the top of his lungs. "Stop laughing at me!" His fingers clung to his ears as he squeezed his eyes shut. "Stop it!"

A cold burst of wind shook him from his thoughts. His eyes shot open, and he gasped, almost like he forgot to breathe. He turned toward Pedro and saw that he was still induced in a nightmarish-type state by the way his face contorted and twisted painfully. Joshua glanced around the train and saw everyone were in their own little dream worlds or nightmare worlds by how everyone looked pained and weary. Joshua's eyes fell upon Teff last as he stood at the front of the cart. His hands remained in his pockets as his eyes gazed around the cart. A look of enthusiasm came across his face as he watched everyone in their own little worlds. When his eyes fell upon Joshua, his enthusiasm turned into curiosity. Teff crossed the train and up toward where Joshua sat. The conductor kneeled into the seat that sat in front of Joshua and gave a charming smile. "You seem upset," he said matter-of-factly. "What's on your mind?"

"Your rules on this train suck," Joshua said blatantly. The anger that he held in his heart made it hard to care of what came out of his mouth.

Teff's eyes widened in surprise. "My, my, that hurts my feelings! I do my best to customize this train ride every time!" Teff stated dramatically. "Why would you ever say that? I believe that my rules are rather fair."

"Uh-huh," Joshua grumbled as he showed his new ticket.

Teff's eyes grew as he stared at the reflective gold paper. "You know, you really gotta have either a real idiocy streak or you are too compassionate, Joshua," Teff said, slightly amused. "Anyone with that ticket is hardly ever redeemable. Why would you do such a thing?"

Joshua met his playful silver eyes with a hard glare. "I didn't. It was stolen when I moved seats," Joshua said lowly. "And I don't have any idea of how to get it back."

Teff sighed dramatically as he leaned against the seat. "That does seem to be quite the predicament," Teff said sympathetically.

"Any advice?"

Teff grinned as he took the ticket and read. He shrugged as he handed it back with the same grin that never left his face. "A man's pride when wounded is an animal that can be taken advantage of."

Joshua only stared at him as Teff chuckled. "That…makes no sense to me," Joshua admitted.

"Think it over. It may help." Teff added a shrug. "Or it may not. It's up to you."

Joshua sighed heavily as his hand clenched the ticket angrily. "I don't get it," Joshua said as an afterthought.

Teff's ears perked at the chatter and cocked a brow toward Joshua. "Don't get what?" Teff asked.

"I don't get you. You are like this devil with some people and an angel for others! Like, you are just this…this…this thing that only cares if you beat your personal times on cart rides!" Teff gave Joshua a sad smile as he rested his head in a hand propped on the back of the seat. "You make no sense! You seem to enjoy all of this!"

"But I do!" Teff admitted happily.

"How? You're like a coked-up Grim Reaper!"

Teff giggled. "Joshua, my job is not to side with heaven or hell. It's not even to be biased toward either spectrum. You forget, I am a human soul just like you," Teff said as his giggle died down. "I was a human like you. Living, breathing, stressing about things that never really mattered in the end. To be honest, this is the best thing that has ever happened to me. Meeting souls and damned or not has always brought something new and exciting! No two are alike on a cart!"

"How do you even get a job like this?"

Teff's happy attitude died down at the question. With a small sigh, his smile turned sad as he glanced away from Joshua. "Do you really want to know?" Teff asked.

"Yeah, I kinda do," Joshua admitted.

Teff paused for a moment. His eyes cast toward the ground in thought before his cheery demeanor took back over. "Then I will tell you at the end of the train ride when you are on your way back!"

Joshua groaned yet relented. "If I ever make it there," Joshua grumbled.

Teff grabbed for his pocket watch as he shook his head toward the comment. "I'm sure you will. You're stressed now and maybe even angry, but I'm sure you'll make it out," Teff admitted as he opened the watch. The ticks of the clock clicked in Joshua's ears. The train conductor hummed as he shut the pocket watch in one swift motion and gently placed it back in his coat pocket. "Well, would you look at that, we're early!" Teff stated with glee. "A new personal best!" Teff hummed a tune as he went back toward the front of the train.

Joshua grunted as his attention went toward the window that beckoned him. What laid before him was a battlefield that only hell would conjure. Carcasses of the dead were piled high. The rot and decay clung to the bodies beneath them as the train rode through the sky. A dark brownish-purple river ran through the terrain of sand and bodies. The sky was dyed a peach color similar to sand with tinges of red for clouds. Some poor souls wandered and scattered around the piles of dead with small sticks or arrows for weapons. They were starved yet had crazed looks in their eyes as they stared at the train. Joshua frowned. The train tilted downward, and he noticed that there was a track made of bone for the train to follow. The train screeched as it hit against the bone but chugged along smoothly. The piles of dead were at least ten feet tall on ground level. Pools of dirty blood formed underneath the mounds of flesh and bones. The train jolted as a loud thud broke through Joshua's eardrums. He surveyed out his window as the train jumped again. Nothing came from what he saw. When he turned around, his blood ran cold. A creature that looked no different than a demonic titan walked and surveyed the landscape.

"Oh my…" Joshua squeaked as he turned his body toward it. His eyes glanced at Pedro and saw the man shook himself out of his induced trance. When Pedro turned to where Joshua looked, he moaned in awe. The titan creature had a gigantic goat's skull for a head and teeth sharper than razors. The body was all bones with bits of flesh that were rotted and could fall off at any moment. A heart beat in the middle of its exposed chest. The train jolted again as it turned toward their direction. Hollowed holes were the only eyes that Joshua could tell. When the creature pointed a long, boney finger toward the train, it roared. The roar was higher pitched and louder than chalkboard scratch. The terror in Joshua's heart made it impossible for him to move. He was paralyzed in place as fear gripped his spinal cord.

"That's insane!" Pedro exclaimed as his hands excitedly beat against his seat. "I wanna fight one!"

"Are you insane?" Joshua questioned, panicked.

Pedro glanced his direction, and it answered his question. Joshua's jaw clamped shut in reply. Their eyes turned back toward the creature and saw that it started to slowly walk their way. With every step, it slowly shook the cart more and more. The sound of excited hands clapping drew Joshua's eyes away from the humungous creature and toward an overly enthused Teff. The train conductor bounced on the balls of his feet as he stared out the window. "Oh, that must be Bunny!" Teff exclaimed happily.

"Bunny?" Joshua asked under his breath. His attention turned toward the titan that came closer toward their train. His heart sped up with each step that came closer to their cart. A boney hand reached out toward them and grabbed the cart. The train abruptly stopped, and Joshua fell to the ground by the force. Pedro clung to his seat with a deathlike grip as Teff ran toward the back of the cart. The train screamed against the hand on it as the horn blew. However, the titan-like demon picked up the train cart. Screams flowed into Joshua's ears as the pressure kept him close to the ground. They stopped moving when they became eye level with the huge creature. Joshua shakily got back into his seat. Fear froze his body once he hit the chair. He heard Teff as the conductor opened the door in the back of the cart.

"Bunny! I knew that was you!" Teff called out. Joshua's whole body shook as if he were in the coldest parts of the Artic circle as his head slowly swiveled toward Teff. "Aren't you going to come and say hi?"

Joshua snapped his head back toward the creature. It did not move, but he saw past it, and other huge titans slowly made their way toward the train. His eyes fell back onto the titan that held them midair. A glint of light shined from the left eye that was closest to the cart. After a moment, there was another glint. He felt his face flushed at the next sight. A creature climbed out of the eye. It had a rabbit's skull as its head and six boney arms came from its upper body. It had a set of legs that rotted flesh still clung to. Guts and heart clung to the spine and rib cage of the creature. When it sat on the titan's eye, Joshua felt his soul want to run away. His body turned to ice as his heart chose to stop beating. Paralysis kept him upright and focused on the creature as the creature waved toward Teff. It seemed like a friendly gesture in Joshua's eyes. "Hi, Bunny! Did you want the souls dropped off here instead of the usual drop-off point?"

The train horn blasted again in protest, and Joshua felt every bit of his being agreed with it. The rabbit skull tilted its head from side to side. After a moment, it nodded. Teff glanced back into the cart happily. "HL 6! Who do we have here for HL 6! I am looking for a glowing ticket for HL 6!" Teff stated in glee. His head turned as his eyes scanned the room. Three people slowly showed their tickets. Teff motioned for them to stand. "Perfect! We are going to let you off here! Bunny will be the one to let you all down with the rest of the mongrels. I hope you all are excited." Glowing tickets were clutched tightly as the three stood. Their eyes remained focused on the titan just outside the window. They slowly shuffled toward the middle of the aisle.

"Shit, I should have switched with someone to get this hell," Pedro whispered under his breath as they watched the souls that slowly stepped out and onto the boney wrist and forearm. Joshua gulped down the bile that grew in his throat. The bunny-skulled creature stood to full height on the rim of the eye socket. With one leap, it joined the three souls on the forearm.

"Have fun, Bunny! I'll see you with the next cycle!" Teff waved before he shut the door.

Bunny nodded toward Teff before its attention went back to the souls that stood before it. The creature used a set of hands and grabbed the first soul by the throat. It used a third hand on its right side and shoved it straight into the chest of a female soul. The woman's shriek ripped through Joshua's ears. A hand on its left side clawed deeply into a man's face. The woman and man were thrown off the arm. Joshua refused to glance down to see where they plummeted. The soul that Bunny still clutched was a younger man that struggled pitifully against the boney hands. Blood dripped down the boney hands as his body thrashed against the grip. Bunny turned its head and leaped back toward the eye socket it came from. It hopped down into the darkness of the eye with the man, and Joshua saw nothing after that. Not even a glint of light passed through the eye.

"Oh, isn't Bunny so nice? He didn't even eat these ones," Teff said with a friendly fondness in his tone.

A moan filled Joshua's ears. His eyes turned away from Teff and back on the titan. It unhinged its jaw as it groaned loud enough that the cart vibrated against the titan's grip. A moment later, the hand let go, and the train dropped. Joshua screamed alongside Pedro and the other man on the cart. Joshua shot up toward the ceiling and slammed against it. Pedro smashed into the ceiling alongside him. The train crashed against the ground with a powerful force. Joshua plummeted into the ground. The air escaped his lungs as pain pounded against his head. His whole body throbbed as pain chorused through him. It felt no different than if every bone smashed in his body. Humming fluttered through his ears as he groaned in pain. His eyes broke open, and the whole world was fuzzy and swayed around him. He barely made out the black spots as feet that stepped toward him. His body refused to move. A pressure held him securely in place. Cold slowly crept along his body as his eyes slowly closed. The humming died down as the cold slowly crept up his arms and legs.

His heart pounded alongside his head. As the cold crawled slowly toward his shoulders and hips, his heart sped up painfully fast. Blood pounded against his head as if it were trying to crack his skull to escape. The cold slowly seeped into his back and chest. His heart continued to go faster and faster. When the cold gripped his chest, his heart slowed down drastically until it barely pumped at all. The pain in his head took over his senses, and slowly his consciousness faded. It faded and faded and faded into the dark unconsciousness that claimed him.

Chapter 16

In the End...

THE WATER WAS PEACEFUL. The clouds covered the sun and dyed the surrounding area in a murky light gray. The area was silent. Joshua walked along the track as his clothes dried against the humid air. Embarrassment flooded through his mind. His feet clunked against the wood of the old train tracks as he crossed onto the bridge. Just a flat piece of track over water, but to Joshua, it brought comfort. His eyes trailed toward the water as anger raced through his bloodstream.

"Why?" Joshua growled to himself. His hands clenched into fists as he turned rigid. His body shook from the tension that built up. A lone yellow feather fell from his dried clothes and down against his hole filled shoes. "What did I do to deserve it?" Joshua asked himself aloud, his head raised to the sky. No answer came to his mind, and rage boiled up inside him. "What did I do?" he shouted as loud as he could. "Really! A fucking prank? When is it a prank to dunk someone in the swimming pool and then dump fucking feathers all over them!" The wind blew against him, and he punched at the air. "God damn it!" He gritted his teeth as he punched wildly into the air. "Why! Why do they even pick on me!" Tears stung his eyes as he lowered himself on the track. He curled his knees into his chest as he sat along the edge of the track. "It's not my fault...is it? All I do is draw and write and, and, and stay low. I don't pick on anyone. I don't bully people to get off." His eyes glanced down toward his clothes. They were a bit tattered and had a few wrinkles, but they were clothes. His heart slowed down as he looked them over. "Is it 'cause I'm poor? Or because I just don't talk a lot? I mean, why? I don't do anything to people. I just…am I just not meant to be here?" His eyes glanced down toward the water. It peacefully laid there and reflected its environment perfectly like glass did. His eyes stared out around his environment.

Everything around him was peaceful. In fact, it was gorgeous to look at. The sky was mostly gray, yet small rays of yellow poked out in the distance. The wind whistled against his body and shook him. His heart slowed down as his mind continued to race. Fear no longer gripped him so tightly as it usually would, and the anger dissipated. All that remained was a heightened sense of loneliness. A hard truth to himself that he was alone. "I guess…no one would miss me if I left, huh?" He turned to his surroundings. Then his hand trailed to his pocket and brought out his phone. No messages. No missed calls. When his phone pinged, it showed he was tagged with other people in a social media post. His head shook in dismay as he placed the phone down on the cracked wood next to him on the track. Slowly, he stood. A cold, emotionless barricade walled up in his mind. His eyes focused on the water before him. His body felt oddly numb. His head turned blank. There was only one thought that traced through his head. *I don't belong here. No one will miss me once I'm gone. Everyone will move on.*

He took a step forward, and his toes curled in his shoes over the edge of the wooden track. He took one final breath. Moist air rushed through his lungs. It was sweet. It felt good. It felt like he was going to be okay. And with that, his world turned black.

Joshua shot open his eyes and sat up in his seat. He gasped for air like he had held it in for hours. His heart pounded against his chest. The ache in his head dulled down into an annoying pang. Tears unconsciously streamed down his cheeks as he coughed. His hand held his throat as he moved onto his knees. Bile rushed from his stomach and up his throat. Nothing spewed out as he gagged. He gulped in air, and his head hung low, and he used an arm on a seat to steady himself. He took huge breaths and calmed himself down.

When he tried to stand, a pressure kept him on his knees. Humming broke the silence against his eardrums. His head snapped up, and he winced against the sudden jolt of pain. His eyes found Teff and concentrated on him. The man strolled around the cart aimlessly. His silver eyes glanced around at anything that may keep his interest.

Joshua turned his attention to the other two that remained on the cart. Pedro groaned as he laid beside him. The other man shakily got onto his knees as Joshua laid his eyes on him. Joshua did his best to stand, but his legs refused to move past the knees. When he looked down, his legs felt weak and as useless as if they were stuffed with straw. Something glowed in his pocket that caught his eyes. His body turned rigid. His hands shakily dug into his pocket. The paper rubbed against his fingers, and he pulled it out. The paper reflected a rainbow-like hue as it gleamed against the lights of the cart. End was stamped in bold dark letters against the white ticket. Joshua shook his head and cursed under his breath. *I'm out of time.*

"J-Joshua?" Joshua's ears perked and turned toward Pedro. His pocket glowed, and a frown cracked on Joshua's lips. Both their time was up.

"You doin' okay?" Joshua asked as he watched Pedro struggle into a kneeling position. Pedro winced as he nodded.

"Reliving your own death isn't a picnic," Pedro admitted.

"I believe it," Joshua murmured in reply. His eyes glanced out toward the window, and something jumped out to him. Nothing was there. It looked no better than if they were in an entirely pitch-black room. Joshua took in a deep breath. Fear gripped his whole body, yet for once, he did not mind. The fear did not bother him this time. His heart did not race. In fact, it slowed down to a steady beat. He was afraid yet calm. At least, his mind was calm enough to think a bit clearly. When his eyes glanced at his two counterparts though, they seemed rigid and afraid. They glanced around, and their bodies shook. Their eyes raced like their minds. Pedro visibly clung to himself as his eyes trailed up to the window.

"O-our final stop?" Pedro asked.

Joshua glanced back out the window. "Yeah, our final stop," Joshua replied calmly.

"A-all right now," the man further away from them spoke up, "time to…time to get a move on, Mr. Teff. Get them outta here so we can get goin'." The three of them turned to the conductor.

Teff stared back at them and cocked his head. A dark smile crept on his face as he motioned with his head toward the back of the cart. "The door is already open. It is up to you to get off. This our final stop. This is station end."

"Y-y-you mean, I gotta wait here till they feel like gettin' off?" the man asked, outraged.

"Should be no problem," Teff said happily. Joshua looked back at the man and watched as he shook under their calm eyes. In fact, it reminded Joshua of that Hollander guy from a couple stations back. After a moment of thought, an idea came to his mind. His attention turned to Teff as the conductor hummed to himself and tapped his foot to the beat.

"Excuse me, Teff," Joshua called for him. Teff stopped his humming and nodded toward the boy. "Do you mind reading my ticket to me? I feel like I am…forgetful of my life. I'd like to have that peace of mind."

A devilish glint shined in the conductor's eyes as he nodded. "Of course! If I may?" Teff walked over to Joshua and held out his hand. Joshua handed the ticket over to the man. Teff winked back at him as he cleared his throat. "Geyorg Hoffsteimer," Teff began. "A man of many trades. Through life, he was a judge. He judged criminal court to be specific. However, he also took many bribes and called in a number of favors. Favors in particular that had dealings with a sex trafficking ring where he would take men and women from prisons that were orphans or immigrants and sold them for a pretty penny." Teff chuckled as he read it aloud. "Oh, the irony. The man that is supposed to help people is the one that sells people. Also letting murderers, rapists, and larcenists go free, especially if they were part of a higher tax bracket."

"W-well, ya gotta make a livin'," the man argued shakily.

"Scum, if you ask me," Teff chided. "A man that deserves to be here in the pit."

"The pit?" Pedro asked.

Teff nodded toward the outside. "A nickname that we give this area here because there is no real name for it. The moment you step out that door, you don't see anyone or anything anymore. There are millions of souls, some of them even right next to one another, and they just don't know it. They are fully desensitized. They lose their sight, smell, feeling, hearing, and touch. Everything around them is no better than an underwater abyss. Even the air here is thick to breathe and fills the lungs quickly. It's almost like the constant feeling of drowning, yet you are getting just enough energy and air to keep going."

"Scum?" the man called out as he ignored the area that Teff described. The man stood to his feet and leveled Teff with a glare.

"Of course," Joshua added in. He could barely move from his spot on the ground, but just enough to turn toward the man. "No better than the rest of the worthless crap at the bottom of the world's shoes."

"I am not crap!" the man shouted back.

"Oh?" Teff raised a brow.

"I was a lawful man! I followed what I felt was right. They didn't have anything to them! They weren't providing to the economy! In fact, they were stealing from it. So what was the big deal if they were gone? No one was missing them anyways. I had a family to pay for! That money went to something so much better than them."

Joshua turned back as Teff's smile grew dark. He strolled over to the man slowly. "So you are Geyorg Hoffsteimer?" Teff asked.

The man stiffened and puffed out his chest defiantly. "I am."

Teff chuckled darkly as he held up the glowing ticket. "Then this is your ticket, dear sir, meaning this is your stop."

Joshua's eyes widened as the man took a step back. Instead, he pulled out his ticket that did not glow. "N-no, I don't. I got this ticket. Got it fair and square."

Teff clicked his tongue as he shook his head. "Tch, tch, tch, oh no, dear sir, you did not ask for the rest of the rules," Teff said as he plucked the ticket from his hand and replaced it with the one that glowed.

"B-but you said if you can switch it, then the person that has the glowing one has to get off!"

"Yes, and I also said that hell has far less rules. No one asked for the rest of the rules to that little game." Teff's smile widened inhumanely as the man clenched his teeth.

"W-what do you mean?"

"The person has to get off the train with that ticket in my hand. If I catch wind that you stole their ticket and you say it before they depart, I can just as easily switch it back so that you are sent to the right part of hell."

Joshua's eyes widened.

"I...but I didn't—"

"You didn't ask," Teff shrugged nonchalantly. "It is a rule that I must follow in hell. Troublesome, I know. It was even more troublesome when I heard someone else talking about how they stole a ticket in the first station of hell." Teff sighed dramatically. "You have *no* idea how hard it is to send a telegram during dimensional shifts, and you all are busy pitying over yourselves." He shrugged in the end. "Oh well, the other conductor told me that it would be fixed during his route, not mine. I guess I got away scot-free with that one." The two stared each other down. "It's hard to cheat hell, isn't it?" Teff asked with a small giggle.

"Why you son of a—"

A low growl cut off Geyorg's sentence. Joshua's hair stood on the back of his neck, yet somehow, he was still eerily calm. "What was that?" Joshua asked aloud.

Teff took a step away and trailed over to Joshua. "You're gonna want this," Teff stated as he held the golden ticket toward him. Joshua took it gratefully and held it as tight as he possibly could. Pedro cowered as he curled in on himself. "This station still has a demon onlooker as a gatekeeper," Teff said as he stood in front of Joshua. "And I have to admit, it absolutely hates waiting for the passengers to get off." The conductor remained relaxed as he sighed. "I would hurry up if I were you two. Wouldn't want to have you all fearing for your lives the way your victims did."

Pedro's body curled into a small ball, while the other man stood. His attempt of defiance was replaced with fear as he shook. A black mass slowly filled onto the cart. It was like slow-moving water in Joshua's eyes. It bubbled up onto the cart and slowly flooded the exit way. It waved toward everyone on the cart. A bitter cold fell upon the cart as everyone watched in fearful awe. The liquid mass slowly crawled up toward the two. When it crawled toward Pedro, a shriek ripped out of his throat as the mass slowly covered him. His eyes bulged open as it covered him like a slow disease that plagued him. As it went up his body, the sounds of bones cracking and breaking popped in Joshua's ears. A mixture of terror and pain contorted Pedro's face. As the liquid got to his face, it slowly poured into his mouth and up his nose. Pedro choked against it, and it slowly seeped through his eyes. As the black mass covered Pedro's head, a distinct crunch emanated from it. The screams stopped, and it slowly dragged the mound that was Pedro away.

When Joshua's eyes turned toward Geyorg, the mass was already halfway up his body. His legs broke underneath him, which caused the man to cry out as he fell forward into the mass. It slowly consumed him, and the distinct pops and crunches could be heard from miles away. Geyorg cried out in pain as the mass gave one final crunch that partially deflated the mound that was Geyorg. A deafening silence fell over the cart as the mound was dragged out. The liquid seeped out of the cart and left no trace behind. Teff huffed as he walked toward the back of the cart.

"You know, you would think some of these demons would cut down the melodrama. I'm supposed to be the dramatic one here," Teff chided as he shut the cart door. The click was loud and distinct as it locked. Joshua let go of a breath that he did not know he held inside him. He surveyed the cart and stopped Teff when he walked by. Teff hummed down to Joshua, "Let me get the train moving before we talk, hm? That way you can stand." Joshua silently agreed, and Teff continued forward. The bell rang, and Joshua felt tears around his eyes. It was the sweetest noise that he ever heard. Teff swung around and looked down at the only person left on the train. "And what did you want to ask, Joshua?"

"You said there were two near deathers on this train," Joshua said. He motioned toward the cart with his arms. "Why am I the only one here?"

Teff looked down at Joshua, and a small smile fell upon his face. "Are you ever going to get off the ground?" Teff asked. Joshua looked down at his knelt position and sprung up to his feet. "Are you going to answer me?" Teff paused for a moment as he contemplated an answer. He tilted his head side to side and hummed as he searched his mind. Joshua felt the trepidation in his chest as he waited, a feeling that he loathed with every fiber of his being.

"You asked me how I became a train conductor, correct?" Teff asked. Joshua only nodded. Teff slowly dug into a back pocket and pulled out a golden ticket. PP was written on it in big letters with a spikey ball on the top right-hand corner. Joshua's eyes widened a bit.

"You see, us near deathers really are different. Y'see, we are offered a chance to witness the afterlife. To really assess our lives and make a choice. Stay or go. If our body ends up being meant to die, we stay, and the top-right corner indicates our secondary stop. For you and me both, that's purgatory. However, if we stay voluntarily, we keep this pass and become a conductor and are given a cart." Teff giggled a bit. "It means in the end, we chose death. And our bodies die naturally, and we are stuck with a constant ticket." Teff paused and assessed Joshua for a moment. His eyes scanned the boy before he continued. "Believe it or not, I wasn't much different from you. The big difference between us was that I was never anxious. I was… guilty. PTSD really never…never sat well with me."

"PTSD?" Joshua inquired.

"Post-traumatic stress disorder. I was…I was abused when I was young. And the memories and depression made it hard to get through the life I lived. We were both dealt bad hands for a beginning, I'll admit that." Teff sighed as his body leaned against a seat halfway up the aisle. "I found you so interesting though. Anxiety was one thing that never really got to me. Panic attacks on the occasion, but never so constant."

"So…why are you here? How did you…end up here?"

Teff smirked. "Would you believe me if I said I was a radio host in the living world?"

Joshua nodded. "You are lively enough," Joshua admitted.

Teff grinned. "Oh, I am a fan of the theatrics. And back where I was from in the 1920s, it was the radio that gave me an opportunity to shine. It was my safe haven, a spot where the guilt and depression never drained me." A smile grew fonder on Teff's face as memories flooded through his voice. "Yet one night, I made a mistake of turning down the wrong alleyway on a particularly long night at the station. I was robbed and beaten within an inch of my life." Teff motioned toward his ticket. "Literally."

"B-but I don't understand," Joshua stated. "If it was a homicide, why? Why didn't you go back and live a full life?"

Teff chuckled. "Because when I am here, the weight of the depression and horrid memories ran away. I became whole. Unlike you, that did not follow me into the afterlife. It faded away the longer I was on my journey. Almost...almost like I was healing." Teff shrugged. "At first, it was all I reflected upon, but the conductor I had took interest in me. She's a lovely woman a few carts down. She was the one that helped me see that there was a lighter side to my life. That I could heal. Reborn, in a sense. And when my train ride ended, she asked if I wanted to go back, go to purgatory, or stay here." Teff chuckled. "You can tell what I picked. I didn't want the constant strain of horror to come back. I didn't want pain. And being here, I haven't had to deal with that pain. I wish it could have been the same for you, but I saw your panic attacks. It must be really ingrained in you."

"I've had them my whole life. I never really figured it as something to be healed but to be able to live with," Joshua explained. Teff nodded. "So...no one was there to miss you?"

Teff's smile slowly fell. "I wish I could say no, but yes, there was. My darling Kylie. And when I found her on this train a few years later, my heart had never felt such sadness," Teff admitted. "But that is a story for another time. For now, we are done talking about me. Now let's talk about you."

"What about me?" Joshua asked.

"Do you want to stay or go? And if you want to go, do you want to go back to where you are now or restart?"

Joshua turned rigid at the question. "I never realized I'd get a choice. I just thought I went back."

Teff gave Joshua a kind smile. "Well, you do get that choice. I am giving you that choice."

Joshua felt his weight buckle beneath him, and his body fell into a seat. His eyes trailed down toward his hands. He turned them every which way and found interest in the veins that poked out. His head swam with the new knowledge that poured into his mind. The thoughts of Madeline and Tiffany popped up in his head, people that he felt never deserved to be where they ended up. Then it went to Clarice and Geyorg where he thought they were the true scum of the earth. Then his memories switched toward his family and how they smiled when they saw him. Sophie's kind voice resonated in his ears. His father's sobs on hard nights came next. The thought of his mother with her degree was another thought that showed in his mind. Then the laughter came. Being shoved into a pool, being covered in yellow feathers, and being called horrid names by kids at school. The bullies and their beatings plagued his thoughts.

Then the idea of a new life sprung to his mind. To forget and leave it all behind. Find something new and exciting. But it could also be horrid and lonely. No one was ever guaranteed a good life, and Joshua knew that well. His body shook at the thought of another life similar to his. And then his thoughts came to the cart. To Teff and his flamboyant attitude. To the nice elderly woman that sat next to him. Then Pedro the serial killer that astounded Joshua.

After a long moment, Joshua sighed, and his eyes trailed up to Teff. The man never moved from his spot, and his eyes concentrated on Joshua. Curiosity shined in his silver eyes. Joshua gave Teff a tired smile. "All right, I know what I want," he said wearily.

"And that would be?" Teff asked.

"I want to go back," Joshua said. Teff lit up at the response. "However, I have a favor to ask." A fond smile came from Teff as he nodded for Joshua to continue. "Can I know your full name?"

Epilogue

Home

JOSHUA TOOK IN A final breath as the sound of train horns blared throughout the train station. Joshua stood and glanced at his surroundings. A sea of people flooded the area around him. Most seemed confused, others seemed terrified, and a few seemed peaceful. There were a very few that struck Joshua as completely mindless. A fond smile grew on his eyes as he looked down at his clothes, a dark-gray outfit that he had not worn for many years. It still fit him perfectly and still was the softest fabric he had ever owned. His hand reached into his pocket as another horn blasted through the air. A slip of paper rubbed against his wrinkled hand. He pulled it out and saw a different ticket from his original one. HN was written on it, and that was all. It reflected against the lights of the station.

"Well, isn't that something." Joshua chuckled as he held it tighter. His attention looked up and saw his train as it screeched to a halt. Air hissed from it as it came to a stop. At the sound of the horn, Joshua's feet decided to answer. They guided him over along with quite a few others toward the cart. The back door swung open, and a flamboyant smile came into view. Silver eyes danced around as they watched the people that lined forward.

"Tickets! Have your tickets ready as you come up!" Teff called out gleefully. Joshua glanced around at the crowd that lined up behind him. They searched preciously for a ticket. Some eyes lit up when they found it in their pockets, while others scowled or frowned. Some scrunched their eyebrows together as they flipped it every which way. It caused a chuckle from deep within Joshua's chest. The line moved slowly as Teff let person after person aboard. When it got to his turn, Joshua gave him the ticket before Teff even asked. Teff smiled fondly at Joshua as silver eyes trailed the back of the ticket.

"Ever found out if you were related to Sherlock?" Teff teased as he handed back the ticket.

"As a matter of fact, I found out that I'm far better." Joshua chuckled.

"I heard from a few souls. So you made an article about me, hm?" Teff asked. His eyes smiled as his head motioned for Joshua to get on. "I appreciate it."

"Well, your story really set a catalyst in my journalism. I should be thanking you," Joshua said as he climbed aboard. The familiar scent of vanilla brushed against his nose as the yellow-tinted light gleamed down on him. When he turned to enter the cart, memories flooded back to him. "Nothing changed," Joshua said to himself as he slowly walked down the aisle. His eyes fell on a seat that sat near the aisle near the front of the train. A lone young woman sat by the window with her eyes cast downward and hair that covered her face. Joshua slowly strolled up to the seat and tapped on the seat. The thud got her attention as dark-blue eyes glanced up to meet his.

"This seat taken?" Joshua asked with a friendly smile.

The woman shook her head. "N-no, you can take it," she stated shyly.

"I appreciate it." Joshua sat down slowly. His eyes glanced around the cart as it slowly filled up. "So you know where you're heading?" Joshua asked as he settled his attention back onto his neighbor. The girl shook her head as she brushed some hair out of her face. "Well, what's on your ticket?"

"Um...it actually didn't make any sense," the girl admitted as she aimed for her pocket. A golden ticket with PP written on the front of it was held up to him. A spikey ball laid on the right-hand corner. Joshua gulped as memories came to mind of Tiffany and Madeline.

"Hey, I've had that one before!" Joshua said after a moment. "Hell of a ticket."

"What does it mean?"

"It means you watch closely and never leave this train," Joshua said sternly. "You don't want to get off at any of these stops, I'll tell you that."

"Why?" the girl asked.

"Teff can explain it a lot better than me," Joshua admitted.

"Teff?" The girl's brow furrowed in confusion as a frown fell on her face. "Who's that?"

"That's me!" a voice sung behind Joshua. They both turned their attention toward the train conductor that chuckled. "The name is Teff! Teff the train conductor! I will be your guide on this ride of a lifetime!" Teff hummed happily as his eyes fell between Joshua and the girl. "Feel free to ask questions!"

"Or not," Joshua added last second.

Teff chuckled as he agreed. "Or not," Teff repeated. The girl stared wildly from the conductor to Joshua.

"He's an acquaintance," Joshua muttered. The girl slowly nodded as she shrunk into her seat. "So what's your name, kid?" Joshua inquired.

"I am not a kid. I'm seventeen," the girl growled. "And my name is Cassandra," she said a bit quieter.

Joshua nodded. After he introduced himself, they talked for a bit. As Joshua found out, Cassandra is from a high-profile family. She exclaimed her lack of interest in their family business and love for science. As they talked, Joshua felt the tension and pressure that radiated off her. It was no different than if he put two tons of bricks on her shoulders. Teff's songlike voice cut through the chatter of the train as he rang the bell that laid on the wall. Joshua raised his brow. "Must've kept it out this time," Joshua muttered.

"Hello, everyone! Welcome to the ride of a lifetime!" Teff stated with glee as he smiled toward everyone. "There are only a few rules for this train ride. Your ticket will glow when you are meant for your stop! Please pay attention. Anyone with two Ps on it stays on the train the whole time. Now people will try to take your ticket. *Do not* let them! You do not want to deal with the station they have to stop at. And believe me, when some realize where they are going, they will do anything to find someone with that ticket." Teff took in a deep breath. "Other than that, I encourage learning from others on the train especially if you have a double P ticket! It may be useful! Outside of that, we are starting to exit the station! So, everyone, relax and enjoy your ride!"

Everything seemed to work like clockwork in Joshua's eyes. From the fields that they passed to the train when it jumped off the track. The sounds of awe and terror that rippled through the crowd brought a certain fondness with those memories. He remembered when Madeline lost her mind about the flying train. When he turned back to Cassandra, her eyes never left the window. She was glued to the scenery that laid before her. Overall, it was a quiet ride into the exosphere. Well, as quiet as any ride would be. Joshua took the liberty as Teff roamed the cart to pull him aside. The conductor beamed when he leaned down toward Joshua.

"Hey," Joshua whispered lowly, "make sure that girl gets past the end."

Teff's eyes lingered on the girl before they turned back toward Joshua. "This is such déjà vu," Teff replied with his usual songlike charm.

"What do you mean?" he asked.

"Well, that lady from your ride asked me to do the same thing for you while you were busy with your head in the clouds just like she is. It's nice to watch past near deathers pay it forward!" Teff exclaimed. A warmth swelled in Joshua's chest as Teff winked. "I'll make sure that she is taken care of," he assured. "Now back to train conducting!" Teff hummed as he straightened his back and continued down the aisle.

Joshua turned his gaze to the window that held Cassandra's attention with an ironlike grip. The nebula crept closer and closer as the train chugged along. A heaviness fell over Joshua's heart as it came closer. "This is it," he said quietly. Awes chorused throughout the cart as they pulled up to heaven's glittery station. Joshua felt the weight of the ticket in his pocket. When he pulled it out, it glowed a bright white with the rainbow-like hue he remembered so fondly.

"Now we are at station HN! Glowing tickets, everyone! I am looking for glowing tickets with HN on it!" Teff called out as his hands clapped together. "I do ask that you all stay in your seats. Guardians will be here to pick you up, so don't get off on your own."

Joshua turned his attention toward the back of the cart where Teff sauntered to. Six other tickets were held up and glowed the same brilliant white as his. A smile fell upon Joshua's face. They were the real lucky ones. They did not need to take this train twice to get to this station. People in white uniforms and winged pins walked onto the train moments after Teff opened the door. Joshua was met with a kind-looking man that stood by his seat. His golden hair and matching eyes glowed against the yellow light of the train. His smile beamed down at Joshua. "Ready for the next phase of your life?" the man asked. Joshua chuckled and got up slowly.

"Yeah, yeah. Give an old man a moment though. Gotta get these bones in check." Joshua puffed out his chest and took a long breath. The angel waited patiently for him. Joshua got into the aisle and was met with Teff's charming smile.

"It was good to see you again, Timothy Grant," Joshua said with a smile.

"The same goes for you, although I do prefer Teff." Teff stood aside and brought up his hand. Joshua gently placed the ticket in Teff's grip. "And it was an honor to be your conductor two times in a row."

Joshua's smile grew softer as he nodded. His attention turned back toward the girl that stayed in her seat. She had a soft smile on her face as she waved at Joshua. Joshua waved back. "Hope you have a wonderful ride," Joshua said lightheartedly. "This train really does give you the ride of a lifetime."

The End

Sometimes there are moments in life that we all hope we could forget and never witness again. Sometimes life throws us blows that we all see as too hard to handle. When life is too hard and there is mud in your eyes, I hope that you read this note and a smile begins to rise. You are worth more than anything else in the world. And even if you do not believe it, just know that I see that within you. No matter what, do not choose to take a free ride on this train before you are due. I would love nothing more than to see you ride it properly and happy with wherever you go.

Remember that you are important and you deserve to take on the world no matter your hand. Cherish the life you live like it's the only one you have.

—With love,
Teff